STUCK IN THE TRENCHES 2

Flush Season

HUFF THA GREAT

Urban Aint Dead

URBAN AINT DEAD

P.O Box 960780
Riverdale GA., 30296

Contact Author on IG: @ifl_huff

Contact Publisher at www.urbanaintdead.com

Email: urbanaintdead@gmail.com

Print ISBN: 979-8-9888415-1-7

CONTENTS

SOUNDTRACKS

Scan the QR Code below to listen to the Soundtracks/Singles of some of your favorite U.A.D titles:

Don't have Spotify or Apple Music?
No Sweat!
Visit your choice streaming platform and search URBAN AINT DEAD.

Currently on lock serving a bid?
JPay, iHeartRadio, WHATEVER!
We got you covered.

Simply log into your facility's kiosk or tablet, go to music and search URBAN AINT DEAD.

URBAN AINT DEAD

Like & Follow us on social media:

FB - URBAN AINT DEAD

IG: @urbanaintdead

Tik Tok - @urbanaintdead

SUBMISSIONS

Submit the first three chapters of your completed manuscript to <u>urbanaintdead@gmail.com</u>, subject line: Your book's title. The manuscript must be in a .doc file and sent as an attachment. The document should be in Times New Roman, double-spaced, and in size 12 font. Also, provide your synopsis and full contact information. If sending multiple submissions, they must each be in a separate email. Have a story but no way to submit it electronically? You can still submit to URBAN AINT DEAD. Send in the first three chapters, written or typed, of your completed manuscript to:

URBAN AINT DEAD

P.O Box 960780

Riverdale GA., 30296

DO NOT send original manuscript. Must be a duplicate.
Provide your synopsis and a cover letter containing your full contact information.
Thanks for considering URBAN AINT DEAD.

ACKNOWLEDGMENTS

I would like to start off by thanking everybody that brought or just read the book and supported the movement. I know yall loving the book, its plenty more to come. U.A.D, thank your slim for giving me a platform and letting me be me. Its the takeover. Its us, fuck whoever aint with us straight up. I want to shout-out all the authors that paved the way for niggaz like me the one's a nigga respect in the book world. ANTHONY BUCKY FIELDS, CASH EVEN DOE I DONT FUCK WITH ALOT OF YOUR WRITERS U DID THAT MOTHER FUCKER WITH THIS LOCKDOWN PUBLICATION I GOTS TO TIP MY HAT TO U. I BEEN READING YOUR SHIT SINCE TRUST NO MAN AND WATCHED U BUILD AN EMPIRE. YOU LIKE THAT SLIM I GOTS TO GIVE U PROPS. AL-SAADIQ BANKS, THAT BLOCK PARTY SERIERS IS THE REASON I WRITE NOW. THEY'RE MY FAVORITE BOOKS OF ALL TIME. ASHLEY AND JAQUAVIS, LEGENDS. THE WHOLE U.A.D TEAM WE HERE AND BIG SHOUTS OUT TO THE C.E.O ELIJAH R FREEMAN. WHATS UP BIG HOMIE LETS DO THIS

MOTHERFUCKER HOW ITS SUPPOSE TO BE DONE U.A.D WE HERE NOW!

HUFF THA GREAT REVIEWS
TRASH WRITERS SECTION

I WANT TO START OFF BY SAYING FUCK YOU GHOST BY ME HUFF THA GREAT. THE TRASH WRITER OF THE YEAR IS A NIGGA NAME T.J EDWARDS THAT WROTE THE BOOK BORNHEARTLESS. A SLIM THAT SHIT IS TRASH. NIGGAZ LOCKED UP WITH ME TOLD ME TO PUT U AS THE TRASH WRITER OF THE YEAR NIGGAZ HATE THAT BOOK STEPYOUR PEN GAME UP WE IN HEAR READING SO IF YOUR SHIT TRASH IM CALLING U OUT ON IT IF YOU DONT LIKE IT FUCK YOU STEP YOUR PEN GAME UP SINCERLY HUFF THA GREAT.

FREE THE REAL. I AINT GOING DO TO MUCH TALKING RAVEN AN YOUNG HUFF I LOVE YALL, TRINIDAD STAND UP, D.C STAND UP, U.A.D STAND UP

O BEFORE I FORGET THE WRITER ROMELL TURKS THAT WROTE MURDA SEASON THAT MOTHER-FUCKER A GOOD READ I FUCKS WITH THAT JOINT NIGGAZ IN HERE LIKE THAT JOINT KEEP DOING YOU SLIM. WITH RESPECTS HUFF THA GREAT. NOW, LETS GET BACK TO THE TRENCHES.

CHAPTER ONE

GUCCI

1:40 p.m. Gucci took over the whole Montana. He was copping the best dope in the city, plus the cut they were putting on the dope made that shit a missile! They were selling nothing but $100 bags of dope, calling it *torch*. Gucci wasn't selling anybody weight except Shooter and niggas in the hood. Everybody was eating. His man, Shooter, was up 22nd doing numbers, selling the dope he was getting from Gucci. Gucci was spending 200 bands for two bricks of dope, plus he was getting fronted two bricks.

Gucci was purpin'. He copped an all black-on-black A8, and he bought Me-Me a 2-door Benz Coupe. Montana loved him and treated him like he was from up there. Me-Me stepped her game up. That money looked good to her. She was glowing, got thicker, and was cutting up! Everybody but Montana wanted some of that pussy, but knew she was Gucci's bitch. She was a big flirt. Niggas knew she was trying to fuck but ain't fuck her off the strength; they ain't want to fuck up that money with the plug.

Gucci pulled up to Montana, and everything on him flooded. Moneybagg Yo was blasting out the speakers as he parked. He had the Tec 22 with the 42 shot clip tied around the Gucci strap hanging from his neck. He looked over at Me-Me; she had on a Saint Laurent dress that stopped at her thighs, Christian Louboutin heels on her feet, her hair done, red lipstick on them pretty lips, nails, and feet, looking good as shit.

"Take them niggas that shit and grab the money," Gucci told her, kissing her lips. She grabbed the bag off the backseat and hopped out the Audi, pulling her dress down over her thighs. She winked at Gucci and walked off to the building.

"Damn, Me-Me," niggas whispered.

"Heyyy," she replied in a flirty voice, smiling. She was walking up the steps and bent over, acting like she dropped something, letting everybody see her phat pussy. Niggas were grabbing their dicks as she looked over her shoulder, grinning, and walked into the trap.

Greg and lil Andy was sitting at the living room table, dope was getting broke down, and they both had on masks. Lil

Andy was mixing the dope and cut in a blender, he looked up, seeing Me-Me.

"Gucci said this half a joint and give me the money," she told 'em, standing at the door.

"Alright," Lil Andy took his mask off and walked to the backroom.

Me-Me sat the bag on the floor. Walking to the kitchen and sitting on the counter, she looked at Greg, grinned and pulled her dress up, spreading her legs.

"Damn, Me-Me, you need to let a nigga see what that pussy hitting on one time," Greg told her, dick hard while looking at that pussy.

"Me-Me, we ain't gon' tell on you. It's gon' be our lil secret." Lil Andy told her, walking up and sitting the duffle bag beside her. He reached under her dress and slid his middle and forefinger into her.

"Oohhh, maybe next time," she moaned as Lil Andy fucked her faster.

Lil Andy pulled his fingers out her pussy, they were soaking wet. She climbed off the counter, pulled her dress down, and picked up the duffle bag. Me-Me blew Lil Andy and Greg a kiss as she walked out of the apartment. She did that model walk pass niggas in the building, walking all the way to the Audi.

"I got it, daddy," she told Gucci, sitting the bag on the backseat. She leaned over and kissed Gucci's lips while rubbing his dick through his pants. Gucci cut the music up as Me-Me took his dick out his pants, sucking it as he pulled off.

SAVAGE AND BUBBLES

MIAMI

Savage and Bubbles pulled up on Biscayne Blvd, parking behind a white-on-white 2019 Bentley truck. Stuntman hopped out the Bentley blowing a big ass jay of gas that you could smell a block away. Stuntman had brown skin with long dreads that hung down to his waist. He was dressed in a Stunt Season jumpsuit, the front of it opened, showing a big ass Y&A chain hanging around his neck. He had on a platinum Audemars Piguet on his wrist, and big ass diamonds in his ears. You could see the handle of a big ass 44 Magnum tucked in his jumper.

"Brother!" Bubbles screamed, hoping out the rental, hugging him.

Savage got out of the car, and walked up to Stuntman. "What's up, Slim? I keep hearing Bubbles screaming Stuntman this, my brother Stuntman that," Savage said, laughing as Stuntman handed him the jay. "You looking sweet and you definitely living up to that shit," Savage told 'em, hitting the jay while looking at Stuntman's wrist, thinking, *you lucky you Bubbles' folks.*

"Welcome to Miami. I'ma show you how we do it in my city."

"Say no more," Savage told him, handing him the jay back.

"Follow me. We gon' have some fun. Everything on me," Stuntman said and hopped in the Bentley. Bubbles was smiling, happy they clicked as they hopped into the rental.

"Fuck you all smiley face for?" Savage asked Bubbles, pulling off behind the Bentley.

"Boy, just fucking drive," she told him, still grinning.

CHAPTER TWO

FREAKY

When Freaky came out his coma, he was mad as shit; he was cuffed to his bed and charged with a body. Freaky was still in pain. He got hit with a 223 bullet, damn near taking his arm off. The doctors told him he was lucky to be able to move it. He had to get 32 stitches in his neck. The bullet went in and out, hurt like shit; he was cool doe.

I need to get in touch with Savage so I could get a lawyer asap, Freaky thought, looking around the room just as Detective Rob stepped in, walked up to Freaky's bed.

"You killed a 17-year-old kid, that's 30 years. We also know you killed Floyd, took his chain, and gave it to Savage.

That's another 40 years. I got a call from Atlanta; a female that says she saw you kill an informant of mine. Does a Russel Wiseman ring a bell?" Detective Rob asked, looking at Freaky smiling.

Freaky kept his poker face. *I knew I should've killed that bitch, Tiana!!*

"I could help you if you help me," Detective Rob told 'em while pacing the floor. "I know Savage and Sky killed them boys at the Popeye's on Naylor Road. I know about them shooting up 10th place that left Peewee dead and Lil D shot up. I know it all, but I need you to help me and I'm going to help you."

"Get the fuck out my face and my room!" Freaky yelled with a heated mug on his face, looking at Detective Rob.

Rob smiled. "I know about that rape you caught when you was 15, you pervert fuck," Detective Rob said as he walked to the door. "I'ma make sure the world knows. They say they rape and kill rapist over in the jail. Have fun." Detective Rob walked out the room.

I need to get a call asap, Freaky said to himself, closing his eyes, thinking about how he was going to get out this situation.

SAVAGE AND BUBBLES

What you doing with all that ass, let me touch it. Moneybagg and Megan Thee Stallion blasted out the speakers. Stuntman,

Savage, and Bubbles were sitting in the V.I.P section at South Beach. 15 bottles of Ace, $500 a bottle, sitting on the table. They were smoking out the pound bag of cookie. Bubbles was sitting on Savage's lap, grinding, high as shit. Stuntman had two of the baddest exotic bitches Savage ever saw in his life sitting on his lap. He had 25 bands, all ones, stacked up sitting on the table. Stuntman was famous in Miami for having the best and most potent coke in the city.

He sold bricks of powder. If a nigga was getting any coke in the city it was coming through him or one of his Y&A, Money-coon men. They was known for purpin', fucking the baddest bitches, driving that foreign shit, and being the flyest niggas in Miami. Slim was that nigga in his city. Savage was looking at one of the Dominican strippers sitting on Stuntman's lap, staring at them big ass titties and phat pussy, his dick was hard as shit. Bubbles grinded harder, thinking she was making it hard.

I should've come by myself, Savage thought.

The Dominican knew he was watching her on the lows. She smiled and started dancing more seductive, opening, and closing her thighs, flashing him that pretty pussy. *He want this pussy and he with Stunna,"* she said to herself. *"I know he got a check."*

Stuntman was hitting the jay already, knowing what was on Savage's mind. Stuntman whispered in the Brazilian strip-per's ear, she smiled, got up, and walked towards Bubbles. Bubbles was high as shit, pussy soaking wet. She was horny as shit, watching the Brazilian walk her way. She bent down and kissed Bubbles on her lips.

Bubbles was still grinding on Savage's dick, her pussy soaking wet as she kissed the Brazilian stripper back, letting her rub her nipples through her shirt. She grabbed Bubbles' hand, pulling her to their feet.

"I'ma borrow her for a lil bit, Papa," the Brazilian told Savage. He smiled as he watched Bubbles and the Brazilian walk off. Bubbles blew him a kiss, her nipples stiff with anticipation. Stuntman whispered to the Dominican stripper, she got up and walked to Savage, got on her knees right in the V.I.P, took his dick out his pants, and started sucking the shit out his dick. Stuntman just laid back, blowing a big sheet of gas, enjoying his night. The Brazilian took bubbles to the VIP room; she laid down and took off Bubbles' pants and soaking wet thong. Bubbles screamed as the Brazilian sucked the shit out of her clit.

FREAKY

3:17 A.M.

Freaky couldn't sleep, he needed to use the phone bad. Freaky didn't want to use the hospital phone because the police was monitoring him. He was just lying in the bed with his eyes closed when the nurse walked in the room.

"Nurse Smith," he called as she checked his vitals, "I need to use your phone."

"I told you 20 times, Mr. Jones… I can't do that," she told him, stepping back from the bed looking at him with a still look.

"Please. I'm just trying to get a lawyer and holla at my peoples. The police already in my face. I'm looking at life, Ms. Smith. I might never go home, please Ms. Smith," Freaky pleaded while glazing at Nurse Smith.

Nurse Smith looked at him and glanced at the room door where the police was sitting. She looked at Freaky thinking before grabbing her phone out of her pocket, sliding it under Freaky's pillow. "You got 20 minutes. If you get caught, I promise I'ma tell them you stole my phone," she said seriously and walked out the room.

Freaky grabbed the phone and turned his back towards the door and dialed Savage's number.

SAVAGE

Savage and Bubbles left the club with the two strippers, Stuntman gave Savage a Smith 5th and ten bands, gave Bubbles a hug, and dapped up Savage, telling him they was going to talk business in the morning. Soon as Savage, Bubbles, and the two strippers got to the hotel they were fucking. Last thing Savage remembered was crushing Bubbles from the back, while watching the Dominicans finger fuck themselves. Savage nutted hard in Bubbles before passing out, his dick still implanted in her.

Savage woke up around 3:20 a.m. looking around, seeing the two strippers at the head of the bed ass naked sleep. He gazed down at Bubbles, pulling out of her as he stood up. Bubbles was still sleep, legs opened, pussy coated white. Savage put his boxers back on, grabbing some gas out his pants pocket when his phone started ringing. Savage grabbed it and answered as he sat in the chair twisting up.

"Savage," Freaky called in a whisper while looking over his shoulder at the door.

"Freaky, fuck is up, Slim? I'm out in Miami."

"Hold up," Freaky said, cutting Savage off. "I got hit up simple city and spanked a nigga. They got me in the hospital now. Charged me with a joint and everything. I need a lawyer asap, Slim. They might move me to the jail tomorrow. The nigga L from up simp hit me. Get with Nook and get the lawyer asap… I'm gone!" Freaky told him and hung up after hearing footsteps.

"Fuck, Moe!" Savage yelled, frustrated as he hit the jay, thinking, *I got to get back to the city*. He got dressed and walked up to the bed, waking Bubbles.

"What, boo? Let me sleep," she cried, eyes still closed as shit.

"Get up Moe, we gone. Shits all bad… get the fuck up!" Savage yelled, sitting the ten bands on the table for the strippers as he put the Smith 5th in his pocket and the Glock on his hip. Bubbles was tired, irritated, and mad. She was cursing Savage out as she hopped out of bed and got dressed, rolling her eyes, and pouting at Savage.

Savage wasn't paying her no attention. Hiis mind was on getting back to the city as he grabbed their bags with the rest of the money in it. He grabbed the suitcase and walked out of the hotel room with Bubbles, just as the two strippers got out of bed and grabbed the money off the table.

"Fuck that, bitch! I got rent to pay," the Dominican said as she counted the money.

CHAPTER THREE

The made man got a call at 7:00 in the morning by his lawyer, telling him to be at her office at 9:00 a.m. The made man got dressed with a smile on his face. He read the paper about Big V getting crushed with the wire still on his chest. "Rat ass nigga," he said to himself, walking out his house. He hopped in his Range driving to his lawyer's office with Jay-Z blasting the whole ride. When he pulled up to his lawyer's office and hopped out the Range, stretching, as the sun was shining, it was 70 degrees at 8:50 in the morning.

"A great day," he said out loud, walking to the lawyer's office.

His lawyer, Katy Blend, met him at the front door. She was

a nice looking, petite, strong woman in her early 40's. She had a beautiful face and nice shape.

"Mr. Green," she greeted while shaking his hand, leading him to her office. "I have great news, Mr. Green," she told him with a smile as she took a seat behind her desk. "All the witnesses on the case have died. I talked to the prosecutor this morning; all your charges have been dropped." The made man shook his head, grinning. His inner thoughts were yelling, *Man, I love Big Mike the Clean Up Man*. Katty stood up from her desk, and the made man stood up too, shaking her hand.

"One hundred thousand will be here for you in 30 minutes. Thank you and enjoy the rest of your day," he told her as he walked out her office, pulling out his phone.

Tyson had just come from picking up 400 bands from T-Real and he was riding out Montana's parking lot when his phone rung. "Talk to me," he answered, riding up New York Ave.

"They dropped that shit. I guess everybody got killed or something," Tone told him, hopping in the Range.

"This calls for a celebration tomorrow at the club. All real niggas and bad bitches coming out. I'm bout to set that shit up now," Tyson yelled excitedly.

"I'm with it, but no wild bitches allowed," Tone told him and hung up. Tone cut up Jay-Z's *What more can I say?*, singing along as he pulled off reflecting to himself, *I'm untouchable!*

SAVAGE AND SKY

5:40 P.M.

She put coca on her gums, switches on our guns,
We can't go for none, bitch, I put that on my son.
Why you shoot him in his back? 'Cause that pussy tried to run.
Get your hand out your pockets 'cause I know it ain't no gun.

Lil Durk blasted through the speakers as Sky and Savage sat in the chipped-up Tahoe blowing gas. They were parked in Denny's parking lot dogged up, waiting on Nook to call.

"Moe, Miami was like that… Bubbles' brother was purpin'. I fucks with the nigga. Slim, I just had a foursome, me, and all bad bitches," Savage bragged, passing the jay to Sky. "We got wild down there. I know the nigga Stuntman got all types of licks… it's money down there, Slim," Savage said excitedly.

Sky laughed while passing him the jay back. "I spanked Slim too, all drako work flushed him," Sky told him while watching two bitches walking pass the truck.

"Stop purpin'. How many times you hit him?" Savage asked, inhaling the smoke, blowing gas out his nose.

"You know my shit say work. You know niggas be getting hit 50 or better fucking with me… stop playing so much," Sky said, looking at Savage with that *stop joking* look.

Savage laughed just as his phone started ringing. "This Nook,"

Sky started the truck as Savage answered the phone.

"They all in the building shooting dice right now."

"Aiight," Savage told him and hung up, cocking the Smith 5th Stuntman gave him. He took the standard clip out and put the 30 in it. "Pull up to building 510," Savage told Sky, cutting up the music as Sky drove up Simple City Hill.

Sky made a right in the circle and pulled in a parking space backing in, parking. The Glock 22 went to his hip as they hopped out. Kids were running up and down the street and Sky saw two dudes walking out the building and bending the corner.

"Ay, boy," a couple bitches called out as they strolled to building 510. Soon as they stepped in the building, Murder looked up seeing unfamiliar faces and him, Roc and Pete upped, pointing dogs at Sky's and Savage's face.

"Who the fuck y'all came to see?" Murder asked, scanning Sky and Savage up and down, wondering who the fuck they were.

"Hold on, Moe. My folks live upstairs," Sky lied as Savage's hand dropped to his waist.

Roc looked from Savage to Sky and smiled, remembering Sky from jail. "Ay, Sky," Roc called, dropping his dog by his waist, walking up to him.

Murder, Pete, and Savage were just watching. Sky looked

at Roc, "When the fuck you come home, Moe?" Sky asked as Roc sauntered up, dapping him up.

"Like a month ago, Slim. I went to the hole when you came back… yo cellie told me the hot nigga got crushed and you made it home."

"No question. You get that shit I left you?" Sky asked.

"Yeah, Slim. Good looking out, too," Roc told him and turned to Murder and Pete. "Stand down, this the nigga Sky I was telling y'all about," Roc told them.

"What's up, Slim? I'm Murder," he greeted, putting the dog back on his hip, dapping Sky and Savage up.

Pete nodded, put the dog back on his hip, and picked up the dice. Pete was down and was trying to win his money back.

"What y'all shooting?" Sky asked, pulling a bankroll from his pocket.

Pete saw the money and said, "Shoot, 20 bet whatever, my dice."

"Bet it," Sky said, dropping a 20 on the hallway floor.

"You still be selling dogs and shit?" Roc asked, watching the dice land on eight.

"Bet 100 on the straight," Pete upped, dropping his money.

"You already know," Sky told him and then told Savage to show Roc the Smith with the leg in it.

Savage grabbed the Smith off his hip, putting his finger around the trigger. "Look, Slim," he called to Roc before he upped and pulled the trigger.

Bang!

A bullet hit Roc in his face, and he fell on the steps, holding his mouth. Pete tried to reach, but Sky hit him.

Bang! Bang!

Pete fell on the steps, holding his chest.

"Don't move," Savage told Murder, jamming the Smith in his face. He took the dog off his hip and put it on his own. Roc was lying on the hallway floor, holding his face as blood poured out of it. Sky took the dogs off him and Pete's dead body.

"This for Freaky," Savage informed and pulled the trigger.

Murder's body hit the floor hard, blood shooting all over Savage's face.

Bang! Bang!

Savage hit him again, observing Sky as they ran out the building. L and Rocky were walking back to the building when the shots went off. They grabbed that fully shit out the grass, running around the corner. The whole neighborhood heard the shots and watched as Savage and Sky ran to the truck bloody. L saw two dudes running, upped, and got to clicking as Savage and Sky hopped in the truck.

Blocka! Blocka! Blocka! Blocka!

Shots echoed in the streets as the bullets hit the truck, breaking the windows. Sky hit the gas, doing the dash out the circle. L and Rocky let off the whole clip at the truck, watching it bend the corner.

"Who the fuck was them niggas?" L asked Rocky as they

ran to the building. Seeing Murder's dead body leaking out in the middle of the hallway, they froze. "Fuck!" L yelled, shaking his head, looking at Pete's dead body lying on the steps. He examined Roc, seeing he was still breathing. Roc was breathing hard, holding his face, blood pouring out like a faucet. "Call for help!" L yelled to Rocky as he ran to Roc. Roc was taking deep breaths, hyperventilating.

"Sky… and… Savage," Roc said between breaths. "Sky and Savage did it," Roc told L as L took his shirt off, putting pressure to Roc's face. "He from 10th place, Freaky men," he whispered as sirens got close.

Rocky grabbed the dog from L and broke out the building. L was still applying pressure to Roc's wound, talking to him, praying his man didn't die on him but with murder on his heart.

"Fuck them bitch ass niggas!" Savage said as Sky pulled in the alley up Chopper City. They wiped all their fingerprints off the truck, got rid of the dogs, and ran up to Dawn's house.

BUBBLES

"Bitch, while you out in Miami playing house with your secret fucking friend you don't want nobody to know about…" her best friend, Whitegirl, said, rolling her eyes at Bubbles. "Tone's rich ass having a big party at the club tomorrow… bitch, that money coming out. You know China's thot ass in a bitch's face being nosey, we going show up and show the fuck out!" Whitegirl yelled, stood up from the couch, and started throwing that ass in a circle. Bubbles was laughing as she smacked it.

"You know we going to cut up. Bitch, I can't wait!" Bubbles yelled, wondering who was going to show up and who she was going to set up for her baby Savage!

CHAPTER FOUR

SAVAGE AND SKY

7:40 P.M.

"Savage, I'm fucking mad at you because you didn't tell me you had a *fucking girlfriend* and look at how long it took you to come and see me… that's fucking wild!" Dawn fussed at Savage, pointing, while he and Sky sat on the floor, passing the jay back and forth.

"You my girlfriend, too," Savage told her, looking at Sky smiling.

"I know I'm number one, Savage," Dawn ambled up to Savage, sitting on his lap, looking in his face. "And you know that, too, right? And why didn't you tell me you like the way I fixed up my house? You look so cute, Savage." Dawn kissed Savage's lips.

Savage kissed her back and scanned around the apartment, seeing new couches, a flat screen TV on the wall, new tables, and she put carpet on the floor. "I like it. You did good, Ms. Dawn."

"Boy, whatever." Dawn blushed and sucked on his bottom lip. "I'm bout to call Mya for you." Dawn pointed at Sky. "She like red niggas," Dawn told Sky before standing up and walking to her room.

"We still gotta find the nigga T-Real and Shooter. He still fuck with Me-Me?" Savage asked, grabbing the jay from Sky.

"I don't know, but I'ma find out asap."

"Say no more. I'm waiting on this nigga Freaky to hit me," Savage said when Dawn walked back in the room.

"Mya's on her way and I need to talk to you by myself," Dawn told Savage, giving him that naughty look, grabbing his hand, helping him up, and rambling to her room. Sky laid back blowing gas, cooling, waiting on Mya to pull up.

ME-ME

"Fuck meee, oohhh yessss… fuck it!" Me-Me screamed. Greg had her bent over the couch, sliding his dick in and out her pussy.

Gucci sent Me-Me to pick up the money because he had some shit to take care of. Me-Me put on a pair of leggings but she didn't put on no drawers. She put on a white T that you could see her nipples through and pulled up Montana. Soon as she walked in the trap Lil Andy and Greg walked up to her. She let them pull her leggings down and finger fuck her. Me-Me's pussy was soaking wet. She wanted that dick! Greg escorted her to the couch, bent her over, and slid into her phat pussy.

"Ahhh… it feels so goood. Shit, this dick good," Me-Me yelled as Greg held her shoulders, pounding that pussy.

He pulled out of her and grabbed her face before putting his dick in her mouth. Lil Andy grabbed her waist and slid in her wet pussy, recording it on his phone as he fucked her from the back while she sucked Greg's dick.

"Shit!" Greg yelled, coming in Me-Me's mouth. He pulled his dick out her mouth, smacking it on her lips. *Slap, slap, slap* was all you heard as Lil Andy drilled her pussy.

"Fuck!" He yelled, pushing his dick as far as it could go in her pussy, nutting all in her. He pulled his dick out of her, grinning. Her pussy felt good. She then picked up the money and walked out the trap.

Me-Me stepped in the hallway, and all the niggas that were trapping in the building listening to her getting fucked began rubbing her titties and her ass, putting their hands in her leggings, rubbing all over her pussy and bare ass. She was smiling as she strode out of the building. Me-Me had a pleased, relaxed look on her face when she hopped in the Coupe.

"My pussy feels so good," she said, smiling, rubbing it as she pulled off.

BUBBLES

Bubbles and Whitegirl were out shopping all day, and Bubbles' phone went dead. She was so tired when she got home, she just dropped the bags on the floor, laid on the couch, and went to sleep. She woke up at three in the morning with Savage on her mind. Grabbing her charger, she got up, cut her phone on, and saw that Savage had texted three times.

"My baby." She smiled as she dialed Savage's number.

Savage and Dawn were in her bed, naked, sleep. Dawn's head was laying on his chest, legs wrapped around him. She was in a deep sleep. Savage woke up after hearing his phone ringing. Savage climbed out the bed, shaking his head as he watched Dawn reaching out for him, curling back, and falling back asleep. He grabbed his phone, answering it on the third ring.

"Hey, baby," Bubbles greeted as she laid in her bed under the covers.

"Just got up. I was sleep. You gon' pull up and get me?" Savage asked, grabbing his clothes, walking out the room.

"Yeah, boo, give me the address." Bubbles got up and started getting dressed.

"Bring me two of my guns." Savage told her as he took a piss.

"I got you. I'll be there in an hour."

"Aiight." Savage hung up, washed his hands, and got dressed. He walked in the living room, seeing Sky and Mya sleep on the floor. "Sky," Savage called, shaking him awake.

"Yeah, Slim?" Sky slurred, peeking at Savage through slit eyes.

"Bubbles bout to pull up, you need a ride?" Savage asked, looking at Mya's phat pussy as she laid on her stomach, covers by her ankles.

"Naw, but I'ma be on top of that T-Real situation."

"Bet," Savage said, still looking at Mya's pussy, dick getting hard.

Sky looked at Savage and smiled, rubbing Mya's pussy. Mya was faking like she was sleep. She'd been up since Savage first walked out of Dawn's room. She was going to get up and let Savage fuck, but she heard him on the phone. Mya laid back down, sliding the covers to her ankles so he could see her pussy, hoping he walked in the living room and fuck her again.

"Let's switch-a-roo vol. 2 real quick," Sky stated, finger fucking Mya as she faked sleep, pussy getting wetter. Savage looked towards Dawn's room.

"Get the phone out," he told Sky as he pulled his pants down, got in a push up position, and slid in her wet pussy.

"Ohhh," Mya moaned as Savage fucked in and out her pussy. Mya arched her back, letting him slide deeper in her. "Savage," she moaned as he sped up. Mya bit the pillow, so she didn't wake Dawn, as Savage slammed that dick in and out her pussy. "Fuck it, Daddy," she whispered. Savage pulled out and nutted all over her ass.

Savage stood up, pulling up his pants. Sky grabbed Mya's head, putting his dick in her mouth. She didn't move from her spot as pussy cream slid down her thigh as she sucked Sky's dick. Sky was still recording when Savage's phone rang. He saw it was Bubbles and answered.

"I'm five minutes away, don't have me waiting, Trey," Bubbles declared, calling him by his first name.

"Aiight," he told her, walking back to the bathroom. He washed his dick real good with Dove soap, washed his face, and jogged out the apartment, standing at the hallway door. Bubbles pulled up, and he ran to the truck. "Give me one of them dogs, boo," he told her, looking around the streets. She handed it to him; Savage ran back to the house. Sky was fucking Mya from the front, pounding her pussy, when he looked back at Savage.

Savage put the dog on the table, nodded, shut the door, and jogged back to the Lex. Bubbles gave him a kiss, put the dog on his lap, turned up Keyshia Cole, and pulled off singing. Savage laid his seat back and dosed off, drained.

CHAPTER FIVE

FREAKY

1:00 P.M.

Freaky went to court and was charged with manslaughter and possession of a firearm. He got fingerprinted, and his picture was taken over C.T.F. His shoulder was still in pain, and his arm was in a sling. Soon as he hit the unit, he put his bedroll in his room, nodded to a few dudes as he walked to the phone. Freaky put his back on the wall, looking around as he dialed Savage's number.

"BABY, I'm going to a party tonight… it's gone be a lot of money in there, too," Bubbles informed Savage as she walked to the closet to grab what she brought yesterday.

"Kill! I need a move, too… I'm down to like 40 bands," Savage told Bubbles, grabbing his phone, seeing an unknown caller on his caller I.D. Savage answered, observing Bubbles pulling clothes out of her bag and modeling them for Savage.

"You have a collect call from Damian Jones. Press 5 to accept."

Savage pressed five, watching Bubbles walk out the room with her ass cheeks peeking out the bottom of her shirt. "What's up, Slim? I dropped that paper off to your lawyer and went to holla at them niggas on the southside for you," Savage told him, referring to the Murder, Pete, and Roc situation.

"I'm hipped, my lawyer coming to see me today. I'ma try to get a bail so be on point. Put like 4 bands on my books, too. I'ma hit you later," Freaky told him and hung up, moseying back to his cell, and looking around the unit, admitting to himself that, *This jail shit ain't for me!*

Bubbles walked back into the room naked. "Come take a shower with me, Savage, I'm horny," she pleaded with Savage, biting her bottom lip as Savage got up, following her to the bathroom.

～

Gucci came home drunk, perked up, and blended off the molly. He fucked Me-Me all night on a bed full of money and passed out around 4:30 a.m. He woke up at 2 p.m. and noticed Me-Me was still sleeping. Gucci got out of bed and walked to the bathroom. He started to piss and felt a burning and stinging sensation.

"Fucckkk!" he yelled, jumping, pissing all over the toilet. He grabbed his dick, seeing green puss coming out. "This wild bitch burned me!" Gucci boomed, steaming as he walked to the room and grabbed Me-Me by her face, pulling her out of the bed.

"Ahhh, what?" she cried, falling on the floor headfirst.

"Bitch, your thot ass **burned** me. Get the fuck out!" Gucci barked, dragging Me-Me by her hair, throwing her in the hallway ass naked. "Dumb ass bitch!" He growled, slamming the door in her face. A few seconds later, he reopened the door and threw her clothes at her.

Me-Me was sitting on the hallway floor crying her eyes out, thinking, *I can't lose him.* People were looking out their doors as Me-Me got dressed. She picked her clothes up, looked at the door again, and marched out of the building, scolding herself. *Damn, I fucked up!*

"Dumb, thot bitch. I should've killed her ass!" Gucci yelled out loud as he got dressed. "I'm done with that bitch, flat-out," he told himself as he grabbed his dog, leaving out the apartment to get checked out.

SKY

I ain't been broke in a minute. Tory Lanez blasted out the Durango as Sky pulled up to Eddie's carryout on Marlboro Pike. Sky parked, put the F&N on his hip, and hopped out, walking to the carryout. He moved up to the line, standing behind a pretty ass, brown skin, Slim girl with some long, sexy, brown legs, standing in a lil shirt that stopped at the top of her thighs. "Aye," Sky whispered in her ear. She stepped back and turned, looking Sky up and down, liking what she saw. "What's up? I'm Sky, you trying to fuck with me for the weekend?"

"You didn't even ask my name, boy," she said, blushing. "My name's Rose and where we going, Sky?" She asked, grinning, pussy getting wet.

"You with me. I got you," Sky told her, looking in her eyes.

"We gon' see. I'ma go. It better be fun, too, Sky," Rose said, staring back in his eyes.

"Say no more," Sky told her as they walked to the counter to pay for their food.

Shooter and his man, Don-Don, pulled in Eddie's parking lot. Gunna was blasting out Shooter's new smoke grey Audi truck. He was parking when he saw Sky and a brown skin girl walking to the Durango.

"That's the bitch ass nigga, Sky," Shooter pointed out,

watching Sky hop in his truck. He looked at Don-Don, grabbed the dog off his hip, and they hopped out the Audi.

"I'm tryna fuck," Sky told Rose, looking at her as he twisted up some gas.

"I'm tryna fuck, too," she told him, grinning. Sky looked up, seeing two niggas running up to the truck, and ducked as shots went off.

Blocka! Blocka! Blocka! Blocka! Blocka!

"Ahhh," Sky yelled as bullets hit his body. Glass broke, flying all over his face. Sky was fumbling for the dog, heart pacing as he laid in the middle of the console, back on the arm rest. He glanced up at Rose and saw her slumped over with a bullet in her head.

Shooter's tec jammed up. People were screaming and running. It was pure pandemonium. Don-Don ran to Sky's door and snatched it open.

Bang! Bang!

Sky upped the F&N, hitting Don-Don all in the face and chest. Don-Don fell in the middle of the parking lot, and the dog falling beside him. Shooter saw him fall, heard sirens, and took off running to his Audi. He hopped in and pulled off. Sky's body was weak from the bullets. He heard someone yelling, _he's alive_ and blacked out, dog dropping to the floor.

LIL ANDY AND PAT

"Slim, I need you to throw me a oz. Slim, I got you," Pat told Lil Andy as they sat up Montana in the building, trapping. Lil Andy looked over at Pat, thinking, *I ain't got shit for you.*

"Fuck no. I just hit yo hand."

Pat looked at him, shaking his head. *I'm supposed to be your man, but you bird feedin' me.*

"Look at this," Lil Andy changed the subject, showing him the recording of him and Greg fucking Me-Me.

"Moe, that's Me-Me?" Pat asked, looking at her sucking dick and getting the shit fucked out of her.

"Fuck yeah and that pussy good. I fucked around and nutted in that shit," Lil Andy boasted, laughing as Pat watched the video.

"Send that joint to my phone," Pat said, handing Lil Andy back his phone.

"Freak ass nigga," Lil Andy told him, sending the video to Pat's phone.

FREAKY

The C.O. on his block came and got Freaky from the T.V room, telling Freaky he had a legal visit. The C.O. escorted him to the visiting room. When Freaky walked in, a tall, dark skin man with deep waves in his hair, and wearing an all-black Armani Exchange suit on with a pink bow tie, greeted him, letting him know he was his lawyer, and his name was Brian McDaniels. Freaky shook his hand, took a seat, and they went over the case.

"I know I can get the murder charges dropped. It's clear it was self-defense on all levels. It was more than 50 shell casings at the scene. A blind man can see you were trying to save your life. Now, you're going to lose to the gun and with the 30-round clip in it. You're dead on that, but this is your first charge as an adult. I know the prosecutor. She owes me a favor," he said, looking up at Freaky.

"Can you get me bail? I need to get on the streets. If you can get me bail, I have a hundred thousand dollars for you. I need to be out of jail asap!"

The lawyer heard the hundred thousand dollars and his mind started racing. "Look, you have a court date in two weeks. I'll have a bond. That's my word," the lawyer promised, standing up and shaking Freaky's hand.

"Two weeks," Freaky said to himself, "the countdown begins now."

DETECTIVE GRAM AND ROB

"Mr. Sky, look at your stupid ass, shot up and going to jail. Your dumb ass just came home," Detective Gram taunted while walking around Sky's hospital room. Sky got shot three times, once in the side, one in his hand, and once in his ear, taking the top of it off. They had to do surgery to remove the bullet out of his side, a lil bit closer he might've died. They wrapped his hand up. Sky was just waiting to get transferred to upper Marlboro. "You shot a guy in a parking lot, you shot Lil D, and you're getting charged for killing the girl that was in your car. That's 100 years right there," Detective Gram told him, grinning.

"Fuck you, eat a dick! Where's my lawyer?" Sky rebutted him and laid back. *This nigga Gram got me fucked up.*

CHAPTER SIX

TONE

Tone and Tyson pulled up to the club at 12 on the dot in a 2020 money green Benz Coupe. Tone paid 100k cash for it and drove straight off the lot. They parked and hopped out, Versace down from their shades to their feet. Jewelry was all over their body, neck, fingers, wrist, and neck. Tone and Tyson looked, felt, and smelled like money. It looked like a car show in the parking lot when they parked.

They hopped out the Benz and were treated like royalty, shaking hands, hugging bitches, getting the love shown that they deserved. When they stepped in the Exits, all eyes were on them, the baddest bitches in the DMV came out to the party.

"What's up, Tone? Them peoples can't hold a real nigga down," the DJ yelled as Tone and Tyson walked in the V.I.P section.

Bottles of Ace were already sitting on ice. Tone and Tyson sat back and kicked their feet up, popping bottles like bosses do.

"Bitch, did you see Tone and Tyson come in? That's real money. Let's go make that money, girl," Whitegirl yelled, excitedly as she and Bubbles finished getting dressed.

Bubbles had on an all-red lingerie piece to match her dreads. The pussy, titties, and ass part were out. She got her pussy waxed that morning. She had her hair done in a crown, red lipstick on, body shining. Her walk was already nasty, a head turner, but tonight she was doing the most. "Let's go, boo," Bubbles told Whitegirl as they walked to the main room.

Gunna was blasting out the speakers. China, Star, and Ke-Ke were in Tone's V.I.P throwing that ass, clapping for Tone and Tyson. Tone was drinking out the bottle, throwing twenties when he looked towards the stage, seeing Bubbles and Whitegirl dancing. He was looking at Bubbles. *This bitch bad. I want that pussy tonight*, watching as she danced seductively, looking at him, biting her bottom lip, looking sexy as shit.

"Who the fuck is that?" Tone asked Tyson, pointing to Bubbles.

China saw who Tone was pointing to, she rolled her eyes and sucked her teeth.

"That bitch flat, ain't she? That's Bubbles."

"Bubbles." Tone smiled, looked at Bubbles, making eye contact, waving her up.

Bubbles picked up her money off the stage, whispered to Whitegirl, pointing up to Tone. She climbed off the stage and walked that walk up to the V.I.P. Tone grabbed his dick, thinking, *I got to have that pussy.*

GUCCI

Gucci went and got checked up. He had gonorrhea. He had to get a shot in his ass and was told to take three big ass pills for a week. He slid up Montana, and him, Greg, and Lil Andy broke down, cut, and bagged up near half a brick joint. Lil Andy, Greg, and damn near the whole hood went out to see "Backyard."

Gucci bagged up 20,000 worth of dope and was walking out the trap when Pat knocked. Gucci liked Pat. Pat's mother was a junkie. He had a younger brother he was taking care of, so when he asked Gucci to throw him an oz, Gucci gave him two oz, told him, "that's you, just re-up with me." At 4 in the a.m. Gucci and Pat were still posted, taking turns catching sells.

"Give me 10 for 900," the junkie told Pat. Pat served him, pocketed the money, and ate on the hallway steps next to Gucci.

Gucci handed him the jay, Pat hit it, reflecting, *this lil nigga don't even know me but blessed my game when my own men ain't give me shit.* He passed the jay back to Gucci, pulled out his phone, showing Gucci the video of Greg and Lil Andy fucking Me-Me. Gucci was hurt watching his own folks fuck his bitch.

"Snake ass niggas," he said, handing Pat the phone back. "Aye, Pat, I'ma make sure you get rich, slim. We just gotta do a lil grass cutting."

"I'm with it," Pat told Gucci, thinking, *fuck them niggas.*

SHOOTER

THE NEXT MORNING

Shooter woke up the next morning, doing the usual. He fired up his morning jay, sat on the couch turning on the news, seeing who got smoked, and choked on the weed. Standing up in shock, he saw his face flashing across the screen and his Audi truck pulling from Eddie's parking lot.

"Shit!" Shooter yelled, running to the window, nervous looking to see if the law was out front. "Damn!" He shouted, running to his room. He got dressed, grabbed his money, his dog, and ran out the apartment with his heart beating rapidly, scanning the streets as he hopped in the Audi. He pulled out his phone, calling Gucci as he pulled off.

Gucci had just met Tyson in the parking lot. Tyson gave him five bricks and introduced him to his lil cousin, Keem. Gucci and Keem chopped it up. He liked the nigga, thinking he needed a young killer around anyway. Nigga couldn't even trust his own folks, might as well have niggas around with no ties to the hood that was willing to kill for paper.

Gucci, Keem, and Pat were sitting in the trap playing *NBA 2k* when Gucci's phone rang. He paused the game, grabbed his phone, seeing Shooter was calling. "Hold up, Moe," he told Keem and answered.

"Shit bad, slim. I caught Lil Sky lackin' yesterday. I hit 'em, a girl got smoked in the process. I got 30 bands and 4 oz's. I need you, Slim. I gotta get the fuck outta town. My face and shit all over the news. And the nigga Don-Don got hit. He ain't die. I know the nigga telling," Shooter vented, shaking his head as he hit New York Ave, thinking, *I gotta get the fuck outta town.*

"Where you at, Slim?" Gucci asked, mind going to over-drive as he turned on the news seeing it was Montana out for Shooter.

"I'm bout to be up Montana in five minutes, Slim," Shooter stressed, stopping at the light, hand on his dog on high alert.

"Bet. I got 40 on me. I got you," Gucci told him and hung up. Gucci looked at the news seeing Shooter's face. He stood up, pacing. *I ain't going to jail and I ain't taking no chances fuck it*, he said to himself and looked at Keem. "You trying to make 15 bands real quick?" He asked and turned to the window, thinking, *I love you slim, but you know too much, and I love me more.*

Shooter pulled on the backstreet up Montana, eyes on the mirrors as he dialed Gucci's phone.

"Yeah," Gucci greeted.

"I'm on the backstreet, in the Audi. Hurry up, Moe. I gotta go!"

"Aiight, I'm coming now." Gucci lied, hung up, and looked at Keem.

Keem left the apartment and hit the back steps, cutting through the alley. He cut through the fence, walking on the back street. Seeing the Audi, he walked up the block, hands in his hoodie pocket around his 5th. He caught eye contact with Shooter, watching as he put his phone to his ear. Shooter put his phone to his ear, looked off, and dropped his head, dialing Gucci's number again. *Damn, this nigga taking long as shit.*

Dialing the number, he looked up and Keem was at his window. Shooter's eyes got big as shit as Keem pulled the trigger.

Bang! Bang! Bang! Bang!

"Bitch ass nigga!" Keem yelled, grabbing the dog and phone off Shooter's dead body, running up the block.

Gucci heard the shots, released a heavy sigh and put his head in his hand. "Fuck 'em. I ain't takin' no chances."

CHAPTER SEVEN

FREAKY

Freaky got medical clearance and was sent over the catwalk to the jail. He walked with his property to NW 1. When he walked in the sallyport, inmates were hanging on the bars, looking, and asking Freaky where he was from.

"The Southside," Freaky replied as the C.O. searched, telling him he was in cell 20. When Freaky stepped in the block, inmates were watching him from the phones, tiers, TV, rooms, and the basketball court. Freaky didn't pay them no mind as he walked to cell 20. Soon as he stepped in, a nigga stepped in the cell introducing himself.

"I'm Budda from Chop. Where you from?" He asked,

hand in his jumper around his knife. *If he say somewhere I'm beefin' with I'ma airlift his ass.*

"I'm from the park but be all over the city. My name Freaky," Freaky told him, putting his bed roll on the top bunk.

"Freaky," Budda repeated. *This the nigga Bob looking for.* "Aiight," Budda said and stepped down the tier.

Freaky stepped out the cell and walked down the steps, leaning on the rail right in front of the first phone, looking around the unit. thinking, *I got to get the fuck out*, when Budda and Bob from 3rd world walked up to him.

"You Freaky?" Bob asked before he whipped and stabbed Freaky in his face.

"Ahhh," Freaky yelled and tried to run. Budda grabbed his jumper, slamming the knife in his back.

"Code blue, code blue," the C.O. yelled in his walkie talkie, running in the unit, spraying mace. Bob and Budda were working Freaky. "Get down!" The C.O. roared, tackling Bob as the team ran in the unit.

"I'm down, Moe, I'm down. Fuck! That shit burn!" Budda hollered as the C.O's dragged them out the unit.

Freaky laid out on the floor, bleeding bad.

"Get medical down here, now! We need a medic, now!" The C.O. screamed in his radio, trying to get Freaky some help.

SKY

A MONTH LATER

They charged Sky with attempted murder and possession of a firearm. They set him back a month. Savage paid 30k on a lawyer for him. The lawyer had let him know because of the situation and it was on the news that he was only protecting himself and she was going to get him a bond. When he stepped back in the courtroom he nodded, seeing Savage and Beauty.

Detective Rob was sitting on the other side of the courtroom, watching Sky's hearing. He glanced at Savage. *You going to jail next*, he mused. Detective Rob had Savage under investigation for Pee-Wee's murder. He was just waiting for the right time to get him.

"The courts are granting you bail. We set it at 20 thousand. You have to pay ten percent. Your next court date is set for June 6th, 2020. That's 30 days from today," the judge notified as Sky got escorted back to the bullpen.

Savage paid the bond, and he and Beauty had to wait five hours until Sky was released. Beauty was heated, mad as shit, cursing Sky and Savage out the whole drive to her apartment.

"Get the fuck out my car!" She yelled when she parked.

"Shut yo crybaby ass up," Sky told her, smiling as him and Savage hopped out the car.

"Don't make me smack you in your fucking face, Sky,

with your smart mouth ass!" She fussed, strolling in the house behind them.

"I'm about to take a shower, get this wild ass jail smell off me," Sky said out loud, walking to the bathroom.

Savage walked in the kitchen. Beauty was right behind him, pushing him to the counter, leaning on him, kissing his lips. She grabbed his hand, putting it under her skirt, rubbing it up and down her wet pussy. Savage slid a finger in and out her pussy as she grinded on his fingers.

"Yessss," she moaned, looking in Savage's face as he finger fucked her faster.

"Savageeee," she screamed, creaming on his fingers, closing her eyes as cum slid down his

fingers. "Thank you, lil boy," she said and kissed his lips, grabbing his dick as she turned, smiling, and walked out the kitchen.

Savage laughed, sucking her juices off his fingers. *She keep playing these games*, he said to himself, grabbing a soda out the refrigerator.

ME-ME

Me-Me tried to get over Gucci but she couldn't. Gucci turned her swag up and paid her bills; he had that real sho nuff money. He was a boss! All them other niggas were just keeping their fronts up. They were fly but broke and still lived with their mothers. Me-Me was stressed out the last month and wanted Gucci back. She was sitting in her car outside of Gucci's apartment, waiting for him to come home.

She was dressed to the T, looking sexy as shit. She told herself that if he took her back, she was going to change her ways. Me-Me watched Gucci's Audi pull in front of his building. She fixed her hair in the mirror and was hopping out, but her heart dropped in her chest when she saw a thick, Spanish bitch with some lil ass Chanel shorts with the bottom of that pretty ass peeking out the bottom.

"Bitch!" Me-Me yelled and hopped out the car, running up to the girl, grabbing her by her hair, fucking her up.

Gucci grabbed Me-Me off her, picked Me-Me up, slamming her hard on the ground. "Bitch, stay the fuck away from me!" Gucci bellowed, helping his new bitch in the Audi. Gucci hopped in the Audi and pulled off. *I'm moving,* he instantly decided as Me-Me laid on the ground crying, trying to catch her breath.

SKY AND SAVAGE

"Wild nigga caught me lackin'. Soon as I looked up, they were hitting. I ducked, grabbing the dog. I looked up and the bitch that was with me, dead. I get hit in the side, I felt that shit," Sky said, laughing as they sat in his room listening to Young Dolph, cooling. "I got hit in the hand but shook that shit off and grabbed the dog. Stupid nigga opened my door trying to finish me, but I upped and flushed him. All I remember after that is waking up in the hospital." Sky told Savage when Beauty walked in the room with a tall, red nigga. The nigga was designer down, looking sweet.

Beauty saw Savage looking him up and down, she smiled and introduced him. "This my boyfriend Dave. Dave, that's Sky's lil friend, Savage," she teased; she was starting to really like Savage. Savage nodded, thinking about robbing Dave.

"Sky, what's up, slim?" Dave greeted, walking to the bed, dapping him up. Beauty made eye contact with Savage, blowing him a kiss on the low.

She keep playin' games and shit, Savage thought, looking at her sexy ass, dick getting hard.

"Same shit. What's up with them licks?" Sky asked.

"Pull up on me later. I got something for you," Dave told him and dapped Sky and Savage up. Beauty waved and followed Dave out the room.

"Fucks up with slim?" Savage asked, looking at Sky.

"That's Beauty's lil boyfriend. He from Maryland. He up like Trump, be throwing me lil licks and shit and soon as him and Beauty break up, I'm throwing his scared ass in the trunk. He up!" Sky told him, cutting the music.

Yeah, I can't wait to throw his ass in the trunk, Savage said to himself, nodding his head to the music.

BUBBLES

Bubbles and Tone have been together for the last three weeks. Tone couldn't get enough of that torch pussy and head. He finally dropped Bubbles off with plans to get some more of that pussy when he finished handling his business. Soon as Bubbles got in her house, she ran for a bath, fired up some gas, and called Savage. Savage and Sky were pulling up in Mike's car lot when his phone rung, he looked at the caller I.D, answering after seeing it was Bubbles.

"What's up, sexy Bubbles?" Savage greeted.

"You, Savage. I miss you, baby. I got the nigga in a hold, we going to be set after this lick. After this we are done, baby, I want to open up a hair salon, my own club, have your kids, and enjoy life, Savage," she told him, rubbing soap up and down her thighs.

"We gon' talk. I'ma pull up later, so cook something for me," Savage told Bubbles, looking over at Sky. Sky was looking at Savage, mouthing, *you a tender dick ass nigga.*

"I got you. I love you, Savage," she said and really meant it. She was in love with Savage.

"I love you, too, Bubbles," Savage returned, looking at Sky smiling.

"Alright, boo," she said and hung up.

"Lover boy ass nigga," Sky teased as they hopped out the car, walking up to Big Mike's office.

Big Mike met them at his office door since he was watching the cameras and saw when they pulled up.

"Young Savage, what's up, soldier?" Big Mike greeted, dapping him up.

"Shit, coolin'. This my man, Sky." Savage nodded towards Sky. "We got 15 bands, and we need all dogs asap."

Big Mike smiled, sauntering back in the office. "I just got a new shipment, take a seat," Big Mike pointed to the chair and disappeared to the back. Big Mike came back and sat the duffle bag on the table, pulling guns out the bag. "I got a couple of them drakos y'all young niggas like. I got F&N's, the ones that take 45 and 9 shells and ones that take 223's, Glocks, Rugers… what y'all want?" Big Mike asked, smiling while looking at Savage and Sky. "All the hand guns cost 500, the F&N's a band, and the one's that take 223 shells, I want 1500 apiece. Give me 2500 for the drako. I got a mac 11 in this joint, too," he said. "I want a band for that, too."

Savage looked at Sky, both of them were pulling knots out their pockets, sitting 15 bands on the table.

"I got bullets and legs, as y'all young niggas say, for all this shit," Big Mike told them, counting out the money, watching Savage and Sky grabbing the dogs they wanted.

CHAPTER EIGHT

FREAKY

Freaky got stabbed 10 times, receiving over 50 stitches in his head, face, and back. He was put in PC the first day out his cell, getting his hands on metal. Freaky's wounds were still sore and hurt like shit, but he was still sharpening him a nice sharp point on his knife. He wrapped it and told himself that he'd never get caught without one ever again. He was just laying back waiting till they came to get him for population. Niggas had him fucked up!

SAVAGE AND SKY

Savage and Sky got four drakos, two F&N's, one mac, two Glock 22's, and a p90 Ruger. They got legs for all that shit. They dropped the dogs off at Sky's house except a Glock 22 and F&N. Savage had the Glock on him and Sky was geeking to work a nigga with them 223 bullets. They pulled out of Landover, Maryland, pulling in the parking lot, seeing Dave and two other niggas standing in front of a black on black 550 Benz.

"This nigga looking," Savage said out loud, gripping his Glock, looking at all that jewelry them niggas had on. He was down to his last couple bands, anybody was on his list.

"Let's see what this wild nigga talkin' bout," Sky told Savage, laughing, thinking the same thing Savage was thinking as he pulled up, parking beside the 550.

Dave and his men were watching the Durango. Dave smiled after seeing Sky and Savage hop out the car.

"What's up, Moe?" Sky greeted, dapping Dave up.

"I'm cool. Savage, what's up?" Dave greeted, dapping Savage up, introducing his two men. "This Money," he pointed to a brown skin dude with a Cartier watch on his wrist. Savage kept glancing at it. He wanted to rob right then and say fuck it. "This Blueface," he introduced the other dude.

"I'm Savage," Savage greeted, dapping both of them up.

"Sky," Sky greeted, following Savage's lead.

"Come fuck with me," Dave said and stepped off the building. Sky and Savage followed him.

"Dave, who's them?" A tall, black, thick, Amazon, bad bitch asked, sitting on the hallway steps with two of her friends getting high.

Savage, Sky, or Dave didn't respond as they all walked in Apartment 1. They heard the girl say, *they both cute but scared* started laughing. Dave strolled to the window and looked out the blinds.

"The nigga Blueface got over 80 bands in his house. I want y'all to grab the nigga. Y'all keep the money. He got some work in there, too. Give me the work, I got an extra 30 if y'all flush 'em," Dave said, turning to Savage and Sky. "We going out to Friday's tonight with some bitches. I'ma text you when we leaving."

"Say no more," Sky said, looking over at Savage.

"Yeah, line that shit up. We on it," Savage told him, geeking. He needed that money.

"Bet," Dave agreed, dapping Sky and Savage up as they walked in the hallway.

Sky stopped in front of the bitches on the steps. "I'm Sky, this Savage," he said, pointing. "If you ain't heard of us, read up or google this shit," he told them, pulling his dick out his pants in front of the girls, his Glock falling to floor. The girls were giggling, pointing.

Dave and Savage was laughing, thinking, *this nigga Sky lunching.* Sky put his dick back in his pants, picked up his

Glock, blew the bitches a kiss, and walked out the building. Savage and Sky dapped Dave up, nodded to Blueface and Money, hopped in the car, and pulled off waiting on the call.

"Bitch, that nigga's dick was big as shit, got a bitch's pussy wet as shit. Next time I see that Sky, boy, I'ma give his cute ass some pussy," the Amazon told her friend, grinning, opening and closing her legs as pussy juice dripped in her panties.

GUCCI MONTANA

10:40 P.M.

Gucci, Greg, Lil Andy, and Pat were sitting in front of the trap drinking. Gucci glanced at Pat, Pat looked back at him, stood up, and told Gucci he was going to catch him tomorrow.

"Lil Andy, fuck with me. I'm tryin' to see you in *NBA 2k* for a band. I bet I crush yo ass!" Pat said, seriously looking Lil Andy in the face.

"You got me fucked up," Lil Andy told him, standing up. He dapped Greg and Gucci up, stepping up the street with Pat, talking shit.

"Slim, my shit drunk as shit on the lows and I got a play to make. Take me up Ivy City real quick," Gucci told Greg as he stood up, moving back and forth like he was drunk.

"Yo shit a rookie," Greg said, downing the rest of his drink. "Come on," he said, walking off to his truck.

"I'm getting in the backseat, lay my ass down," Gucci informed, hopping in the backseat, laying back.

"Yo shit ain't drinkin' with me no more, and don't throw up in my shit. I just bought this truck," Greg stated, starting the truck, and pulling off. He drove down New York Ave., stopping at the light.

"I got a new shipment coming in tomorrow, so get that paper ready," Gucci slurred, talking like he was drunk, making small talk as he took the .357 from under his Dior hoodie. "You hear?" Gucci told him, leaning up in the middle of the console, .357 in his hand, heart speeding up as Greg parked. "You snake ass nigga."

"What?" Greg asked, confused, turning towards Gucci and saw a flash.

BOOM!

Gucci pulled the trigger. Blood flew all over the window, the steering wheel, and on Gucci's face. Greg's face fell on the horn.

Beeeppppppp was all you heard as Gucci jumped out the truck, sprinting up the block, leaving his cousin Greg slumped over in his truck with his brains all over the windows.

"LET'S GET SOME GAS FIRST," Pat told Lil Andy as they cut through the alley, heading to the weed man.

"Hold up," Pat said, bending down, tying his shoe so Lil Andy could walk in front of him.

"Hurry up, Moe," Lil Andy told Pat, looking around the alley.

Pat grabbed his mini 5th off his hip on the lows, stood up, and pointed it in Lil Andy's face. Lil Andy was in shock, looking down the barrel, thinking, *not my best friend.*

"You shoulda gave me that oz." Pat pulled the trigger.

BOOM!

Lil Andy fell to the ground, slump. Pat ran up, standing over Lil Andy flushing him.

Boom! Boom! Boom!

He turned and broke up the alley, thinking, *Fuck a friend. I rather get rich!!!*

SKY AND SAVAGE

Savage looked at his watch seeing it was 1:40 a.m. He looked over at Sky, and Sky had his seat laid back, F&N on his lap, waiting on Dave to call. They were sitting in Friday's parking lot waiting. Dave, Blueface, and two bad Maryland bitches were sitting in Friday's eating and drinking. The two girls were nice and tipsy off the drinks, stomach full, eyes glossy, and ready to fuck.

"I'm ready," Dave's date whispered in his ear, rubbing his dick through his pants.

"Call the waiter, get the check. I'm bout to take a piss,

then we gone," Dave told Blueface as he got up from the table, pulling out his phone, texting Sky, before stepping in the bathroom and taking a piss.

Dave: *Bout to leave. We in a white Lex truck. Be ready.*

Sky let Savage read the text. Savage started the car and pulled off, circling through the parking lot until he saw the Lex truck. Dave and his date walked out the restaurant arm in arm. They both got in the front while Blueface and his date hopped in the back. Soon as the doors closed, Blueface's date took his dick out his pants, putting it in her mouth. Dave's date took his dick out his pants, jerking it as he pulled off.

Soon as his dick got hard, she switched her hands to her mouth as he stopped at the red light. Savage and Sky put their masks on. Savage saw the truck and watched Blueface hop in the backseat. Savage pressed down on the gas petal and pulled right by the truck, hitting the breaks.

Skuuurt!

Sky was out the car; he ran and snatched the backdoor open. Everybody was in shock, scared to death as Sky put the F&N in Blueface's face. Sky pulled him out the truck, and Blueface's dick was still hanging out his pants as Sky forced him in the car.

Sky hopped in, shutting the door. Savage pulled off as Sky took all Blueface's jewelry off him.

"Where the bag at?" Sky asked, pressing the F&N against Blueface's mouth. Blueface was shaking, heart racing.

"It's in the house," Blueface said, giving him the address.

"Oh, my Goddd!" the two girls cried, still shook up as they jumped out the truck, crying, calling police.

Dave was still in shock, heart drumming. Shit happened fast even though they set the play, that shit scared the shit out of him. Savage and Sky came up on 95 bands, 6 bricks, and 60 thousand worth of jewelry. They crushed Blueface, all face shots and got the fuck what they wanted with that extra 30 bands.

CHAPTER NINE

2 DAYS LATER

7:00 A.M.

Tyson re-up'd yesterday so he was out early making his rounds. He slid up town and holla at V, he made a couple more stops up town then slid up Montana. He hit Gucci with three bricks and fronted him three. He was riding around with over a *"M"* in the car. China was in the neon dropping off the work. Tyson slid out Landover and met up with Money and Dave.

Money was still fucked up about what happened to his man, Blueface, plus, he had his work in Blueface's house, so he took a big L. Tyson just fronted them that shit and the plug wanted his money. Dave and Money hopped in Tyson's car, and Tyson looked at Dave.

"Look, I heard what happened to Blueface, so I holla at the big man. Just give us 300 for that other shit and I got 3 about to pull up when I leave," Tyson said, looking at both of them.

"Bet," Dave said, thinking about the free bricks he just came off with.

"Ay, I'm looking for a lil dude, they call him Savage. He be robbing and shit. It's a nice ticket on the lil dude's head… if y'all run into someone that knows him, hit me," Tyson said and dapped both of them up, watching them get out his car.

Dave and Money didn't speak on it but both of them was thinking the same thing. *Is this nigga, Savage, Sky's man, the one Tyson looking for?* as they watched the Neon pulling in the parking lot.

GUCCI

The hood was hurt, fucked up, grieving when they found out Greg and Lil Andy got killed. Gucci and Pat played the role like they were fucked up, too. Gucci threw a R.I.P Greg and Lil Andy block party. They bought cases of liquor, food, and fireworks. The hood loved them for that.

The next day it was business as usual. Pat became Gucci's right-hand man, touched his first brick, and Me-Me was stressing. She lost weight, skin was looking rough, her lips black from smoking too much.

She wanted Gucci back. Gucci moved the Spanish girl, Re-Re, in and it took everything in her not to kill both of them. She told herself if she couldn't have him, nobody could as she pulled off, headed home, tears rolling down her cheeks.

L AND ROCKY

Roc died in the hospital a month after he got shot in the face. L and Rocky kicked down Nook's door, coming to kill him and his sister. Everything was gone when they got there. Before Roc died, he told them that Sky was from 10th place. L and Rocky was sliding up there every day, but nobody saw Savage or Sky. L promised when he caught Savage, Sky, or Freaky on the streets or jail, he was killing them, flat-out!

FREAKY

5:00 P.M.

Freaky got signed out of P.C. and moved to N.W.2. He had the knife in his shoe. When he strode in the sallyport, he saw the block was on lockdown. The C.O. opened the sally-port, Freaky walked on the unit, people were standing at their cell doors watching him walking to cell 60. The door popped, Freaky ambled in, seeing his cellie sitting on his bunk.

"What's up, Slim? I'm Freaky," Freaky greeted, sitting his

bed roll on the table, checking his celly's temperature. "Where you from?" He told him, watching his reaction.

"Freaky?" His cellie asked, thinking about where he heard that name from. Freaky sat on the toilet and was acting like he was fixing his shoe but really grabbing his knife.

"I'm Font'e, I'm from G-rod. You just got busted down N.W.1, right?" Font'e asked, watching Freaky.

"Yeah, why, what's up?" Freaky asked, sliding the knife in his sleeve as he stood.

"Nigga, Tyson put a ticket on your head, slim. Be on your heels," Font'e told him, thinking this nigga lunching coming on the block. "And it's some niggas trying to see you about their man Killa and I guess your men killed three of their men like a month ago. Shit ain't looking good for you, flat out!" Font'e told him, sitting back on his bed. "You dogged up, slim?" Font'e asked, grabbing his knife from under his pillow. "Cause you gonna have to go straight at them niggas when the doors pop or they going to blow you up. I don't fuck with nobody but niggas up my end, but I've been out numbered before you and for you to know the odds against you tryna die or you tough as shit," Font'e said, laughing. "They pop doors in like 30 minutes, I'ma let you know who's who, but you got to deal with your own shit," Font'e said, giving Freaky law on where all his Opps were at on the tier.

SAVAGE AND SKY

5:45 P.M.

Savage and Sky split 125 bands, getting 62 bands a piece, they gave Beauty the other band. Dave came and picked up the other bricks, letting them know he had another move. Dave never put them on point that Tyson was looking for a nigga name Savage. After Dave left, Savage and Sky went to Big Mike's car lot where Sky dropped 20 on a 2016 Audi truck, black on black joint with light tints on it. They rode back to Beauty's apartment complex, Savage parked his car and hopped in Sky's truck. Sky was twisting up when his phone started ringing. Sky sat the weed on the dashboard, he showed Savage the caller I.D., smiling as he answered.

"Yeah," Sky answered, putting the phone on speaker as he grabbed the J and finished twisting it up.

"Sky, I need to see you," Me-Me told him as she paced the floor. She knew all about Sky and Gucci's beef. She was emotional, mad, feelings hurt. She told herself that since Gucci didn't want her, she wanted him dead!

"Alright, I'ma pull up. That head still troch?" Sky asked.

"Pull up and see me," Me-Me told him, blushing, pussy getting wet. Me-Me hadn't been fucked since Gucci put her out and she got that checkup.

"I'll be there," Sky told her and hung up. "Get her

dumbass to pull the play on Gucci or crush her and make him come find us," Sky said, hitting the j and laughing.

"I'm bout to take a piss real quick, I'll be right back," Savage told him, hopping out the truck, walking to Beauty's apartment.

Beauty was sitting in her window, watching the parking lot bored and saw when Savage and Sky pulled up. "He got a new truck, bad ass," Beauty said, smiling to herself. When she saw Savage hop out the truck by himself, she smiled as she took off her thong and ran to the front door in just her tank top. She snatched the door open just as Savage was walking in. "What you want?" She asked, looking in Savage's face as she closed the door behind him. He looked Beauty up and down. She had her tank top rolled up at her stomach, all pussy, legs, and thighs were showing. "What you looking at, lil boy?" She teased, opening and closing her pussy lips, watching him watch her.

Savage's dick was rock hard. He tried to walk around her, but she pushed him against the wall. "You want to play?" Savage asked. Grabbing her, he picked her up by her ass, laying her on the floor as he pulled his dick out his pants.

Beauty was acting like she was trying to get away. Savage pent her down, sliding into her pussy as deep as his dick could go.

"Ohhh," she moaned as he grinded, digging deep in her tight, warm, gushy pussy. "Savageeee," she moaned, pulling him deeper in her, grinding back on his dick. He grabbed her shoulders and started pounding her pussy. Pulling her to him with every stroke. "Ahhh, yessss, it's deep, Savage, fuck meee," she screamed, putting her legs in a wide V, letting him slide in her deeper. "Savage, O my Savageeee!" She yelled and creamed all over his dick.

Savage came right after her, nuttin' deep in her pussy, collapsing on top of her. Beauty kissed his face, his lips, sucking on his neck. She was in bliss. Savage pulled out of her, pulled up his pants, and went to take a piss. He walked back into the living room, and Beauty was still laying in the same spot with her legs cocked open, thick nut cream sliding down her thighs.

"I love you, lil boy," Beauty said in a whisper, watching Savage walk out the apartment. *He fucked the shit outta me*, Beauty yelled, getting up on shaky legs, walking to her room to take a nap.

Sky's eyes were blood shot red. He was high as shit when Savage hopped back in the truck. Savage grabbed the Glock from under his seat, putting it on his lap, and looked over at Sky.

"Slim, you my man and I ain't into keeping secrets. I just hit Beauty, slim," Savage told Sky, praying he ain't fuck up their bond.

"I'm hipped. She told me she liked you. I just wanted to see if you was going to be a snake or let a nigga know. I fucks with you, slim," Sky said, dapping Savage up. "I'm hungry as shit. Let's go eat first, then pull up to Me-Me's joint," he said, pulling off, cutting up the music.

FREAKY

5:55 P.M.

At 5:55 p.m. the cell doors popped open on the tier. Freaky had his hands in his jumper, hand around his knife. He was hip to who was who. Font'e grabbed his shower clothes, nodded to Freaky, and walked out the cell. Inmates were watching as Freaky stepped out the cell. The tension was thick in the air. Freaky glanced around the unit, walking down the steps, with his hand gripped tight around his knife. He looked to the top tier and watched three people standing on the rail watching him with mugs on their faces. Freaky was nervous, but he wanted to work at the same time, talking to himself, saying, *niggas got me fucked u!* The whole unit got quiet as they watched from the tears and phone observing the three inmates walking Freaky's way. Freaky's heart rate sped up as they walked up to him.

"Your name Freaky?"

Freaky took a step back, whipped, and stabbed the dude talking in his face.

"Ahh!" He screamed as Freaky grabbed him by the jumper, slamming the knife in his head. The other two inmates pulled out their knives, as Freaky fucked the dude that was talking around with his knife.

The C.O. hit the deuces, running to the top tier, spraying his mace. "Get down, get down!" He yelled, spraying the two inmates that were stabbing Freaky in his head and back.

"Ahhh!" Freaky yelled, swinging his knife, blood and mace getting in his eyes. The team ran in the unit, slamming everybody on the floor. "Ahhh, fuck y'all!" Freaky screamed, bleeding as he got dragged out the unit.

"Lockdown, Lockdown!" The C.O.'s yelled, calling for medical attention for the guy Freaky stabbed up. He was laying on the ground leaking out.

Font'e hopped out the shower, going to his cell, saying to himself, "slim worked," laughing, thinking about the nacho he was about to make.

CHAPTER TEN

Savage and Sky circled Me-Me's parking lot three times before they hopped out their truck, hands gripped tight on their dogs. They weren't doing no lackin' as they walked to Me-Me's apartment. When Me-Me opened her apartment door, you could see stress written all over her face. Her lips were black from too much smoking. She was so skinny, the once sexy body she had was gone.

Savage was looking at her like, "Uhhh, I'm not putting my dick in her, she look sick." Sky got his dick sucked and after he came in her mouth, he asked what was up with Gucci and Shooter.

"Shooter got killed. It was all over the news and fuck

Gucci, he tryna play with me like I'm nothing. Bitch ass nigga got a new bitch, ugly bitch, and everything," Me-Me said, rolling her eyes, pacing, emotions racing.

"Do you know where the nigga live? We got 10 bands for the address, I know you know it," Sky looked at her, thinking, *if you don't give it to me the easy way, we could make this shit hard.* He glanced at Savage; Savage was thinking the same thing.

Me-Me stopped and peered at Sky. "Fuck Gucci. I know where he live at. You gon' give me the money, right?"

Savage and Sky looked at each other then looked at her. "We got you!"

CHINA

7:40 P.M.

"Uhhh, ugly ass bitch. I don't see what Tone see in her," China told Star as they watched from the bar, seeing Tone and Bubbles walk out the club hand in hand.

"Fuck Tone's old ass. I want the other nigga I saw Bubbles in here with a couple months ago," Star said smiling, thinking about Savage.

"Who bitch?" China asked, looking at her wanting to know.

"Some young nigga name Savage. I haven't seen him since that night but bitch, fuck what Bubbles talking bout, I'm taking him," Star stated, got up, and walked away from the bar.

"Savage, I keep hearing that name. I'ma find out," China said to herself as she sipped her drink.

TYSON

8:50 P.M.

"You like that Bubbles bitch, huh, slim?" Tyson asked, handing Tone two bags of money as they stood in Auto Zone parking lot. Bubbles was sitting in Tone's passenger seat, acting like she was texting, but was watching them the whole time.

"Yeah, I like the lil bitch, slim. You know I'm getting old; the bitch got a good head on her shoulders. I like her energy," Tone told him, putting the bags in the backseat.

"I just came from seeing Bob. Him and the nigga Budda busted Freaky's ass. I dropped some cash on their books. The word out he can't walk. I holla at my C.O. bitch about him. He got stabbed again, bitch ass nigga in P.C. right now," Tyson told him as he looked around, checking his surroundings.

"Cool, get some info on the nigga Savage. I'm gone, hit my phone," Tone told him, dapping him up.

"Alright, don't let that young pussy hurt you," Tyson said, laughing. He nodded at Bubbles and walked to his car.

Tone laughed, hopping in the car.

"Let's go ear," Bubbles said as Tone pulled out the parking lot thinking, *I got his old ass.*

GUCCI

10:50 P.M.

Gucci had a good day. He made a cool 200, bought a couple bricks of coke and was posted up with the young niggas, selling all 50's hand to hand. It was 10:45p.m. when he finally left. He had the mac on him with 200 cash in the car. He circled the block three times before he pulled in his parking lot. He saw the Tahoe parked in front his building but didn't see no one in the truck. He felt a lil funny, he didn't know why but shit ain't feel right.

He checked the clip on his mac, putting the strap around his neck, he grabbed the money with his left hand and hopped out the Audi. Savage and Sky were sitting in Gucci's building, waiting. They saw the Audi pull up, they pulled their dogs out and were posted on the side of the hallway door, waiting to flush his ass. Gucci was feeling funny, watching everything. When he walked in his building, he saw a shadow and a head peeking out the hallway window.

Gucci upped the mac and got to hitting at the building door as he back peddled to his car.

Bang! Bang! Bang! Bang! Bang!

Shots went off, bullets were hitting the building door,

knocking chips off bricks. Savage and Sky were ducked down, hiding on the side of the wall as 45 bullets flew through the door, hitting the steps. Soon, the shooting stopped. Savage and Sky ran out the building, and Gucci was hopping in the Audi, Savage and Sky ran up clicking.

Boom! Boom! Boom! Boom! Boom!

Glass broke as bullets hit Gucci all in his face, body, and everywhere. Sky was about to run up and finish him when they heard sirens getting closer. People were coming out their house, investigating the shooting. Savage grabbed Sky and ran to the truck, hopping in, getting the hell out of there. Police found Gucci bleeding out, unconscious with a mac and 200 bands in his car.

CHAPTER ELEVEN

Freaky went to court July 7th, 2020, and got a bond just like his lawyer promised. They wanted 10% of 30 bands, he had four bands on his books from Savage already. Soon as Freaky got released his lawyer dropped him off at his apartment. Freaky gave him 150 thousand cash. One hundred for the bond and an extra 50 to never repeat where he lived and to change all his paperwork to homeless. Freaky felt something big was about to happen.

He didn't trust nobody and didn't let anyone know he was home. He bought him a low-key Honda Accord and pulled up Trinidad, copping an oz of crack from Po. He jogged straight to his landlord apartment, hopped out, and knocked on her door.

"Hold on," Mrs. Jones yelled, walking to the door, opening it, and seeing Freaky standing there.

"Can I have a word with you please, Mrs. Jones?" Freaky asked.

"Hurry up! My stories on," she told him, stepping to the side, letting him in the house. Mrs. Jones shut the door, turned to Freaky and said, "talk."

Freaky looked at her in her eyes. Mrs. Jones had on some grey sweats and a white T-shirt. No bra on, big titties showing. "I need a favor," Freaky walked up to her, pulling out the oz of crack. Mrs. Jones looked at it, nipples getting hard, pussy getting moist. "I need an apartment off the books, can't nobody know about it," Freaky ran his fingers around her titties and down her ass, sliding them in her sweats.

Mrs. Jones grabbed the crack out his hand, spreading her legs as he put his fingers in her draws, rubbing her hairy pussy. "You can't tell nobody," Mrs. Jones moaned as Freaky pulled her pants and drawers down to her ankles. He made her bend over, putting her hands on the wall as he pulled down his pants, sliding his dick in her pussy. "Ohhh," Mrs. Jones moaned, closing her eyes, loving that young dick and good crack.

ME-ME

11:50 A.M.

"I hope y'all didn't kill him. I fucked up. I should've never told y'all where he lived, I fucked up," Me-Me cried, frustrated as she paced her living room.

"Chill out, Moe, fuck," Sky cussed, standing up, looking at Savage.

Crush her ass, Savage mouthed, hand going to his hip, watching as Sky walked up to Me-Me, grabbing her around her waist.

"Shit ain't nothing, ease up," Sky told Me-Me, kissing her so her back was facing Savage.

Savage took the dog off his hip and stood up, walking up to Me-Me. Me-Me was crying on Sky's shoulders as he rubbed her pussy. Sky eyed Savage took his hands out of Me-Me's pants, and backed up. Savage put the dog to the back of Me-Me's head and pulled the trigger before she could scream.

Pop!

She fell face first, hitting the floor hard, blood pouring out her head.

"Dumb ass bitch," Savage said as him and Sky wiped down everything they touched. "She was going to tell," Savage voiced as they walked out the apartment, closing the door back like everything was normal.

"I'm hipped, fuck that bitch. Let's go get something to eat," Sky said as they hopped in the truck and pulled off like ain't shit happened.

TIANA

Tiana told the prosecutor everything she knew about the murder except her role. The prosecutor from ATL got in touch with the prosecutor from D.C., they went to a grand jury with the information Tiana provided and was ready to charge Freaky with Russel's body. Detective Rob and Gram got the information and were happy as hell. They went to jail personally to deliver the news and was shocked, hurt, and confused that Freaky was released on bond. They were even more upset that they didn't have an address for him.

The two detectives rushed back to the station with the lab test back from the semen found in 14-year-old Tiana's body. When they saw Freaky's name they were in shock.

"Put his face all over the news. It's a $200,000 dollar reward for any information on his whereabouts. Let's take this pervert down," Detective Rob yelled, grabbing his coat, rushing out the room.

FREAKY

2:03 P.M.

Freaky was in his apartment packing some of his clothes, getting high, when the news caught his eye.

"We are reporting live from D.C. News. Police have an outstanding warrant out for Damian Jones, age 24, in

connection with the rape and murder of 14-year-old Tiana Smarts and her mother, Amanda Smarts. He is also pending trial for the murder of 17-year-old Danny Law. It's a $200,000 reward for his arrest. He is armed and dangerous, so proceed with caution. If you have any information, please contact 1-800-Crime-Stoppers."

Freaky ain't panic, he just shook his head. Standing up off the floor, he walked to his room, grabbed his dog, and left out the apartment. When he stepped out and was walking out the building, Pam and her father were walking in. Pam had been looking for Freaky for the last three weeks. She wanted to tell him her big surprise but couldn't because she was with her father. Freaky greeted both of them and left the building.

"Oh my God," Mrs. Jones gasped, covering her mouth after seeing Freaky's face on the news. "I'm turning his perverted ass in now," Mrs. Jones said to herself, grabbing her phone when she heard a knock at the door. "Who is it?!" She yelled, rushing, wanting to let the police know where Freaky lived. She snatched the door open and saw a flash.

Pop! Freaky pulled the trigger, shooting Mrs. Jones in the head. He turned and ran out the building, promising himself he wasn't going back to jail.

CHAPTER TWELVE

"*D*amn, your man did some wild shit, Bob. I ain't even know he was home," Sky told Savage, handing him the J.

"Damn," Savage replied, hitting the J, blowing gas in the air, watching the news. Beauty walked in the living room in an all-grey sundress that looked painted on. Her hair was done in curls, hanging to her shoulders. She had red lipstick on her pretty, full lips.

"Move," she told Sky, pushing his head, walking to Savage, sitting on his lap. "Who is that?" She asked, pointing to the T.V., noticing Freaky's face, and hearing it was a manhunt out for him.

"A good man in a fucked-up situation," Savage told her, handing Sky back the J.

"Me and Savage going out, Sky. I don't know what you

about to do, you need to find you a girlfriend or something," Beauty said, grabbing Savage's hand, walking him to the door.

"Alright, slim," Savage shouted to Sky as he and Beauty journeyed out the door. Sky finished off the weed and stood up.

"I'm bout to get me a couple bitches, fuck you talkin' bout," Sky said out loud, walking to his room to throw on some dripping shit.

TONE

7:10 P.M.

"Look at this wild nigga," Tone snarled, shaking his head in disgust as Bubbles sat on his lap, watching the news, catching the manhunt out on Freaky. Bubbles was in shock after spotting Freaky's face all over the news, hoping Savage was okay. "That's why I put money on that sucka's head, him, *and* his man Savage. Niggas like that don't suppose to walk on this earth," Tone said out loud, but more to himself venting.

Bubbles' mind was racing, she needed to get his ass before something happened to Savage. She knew all Tone's routines, but she was just waiting for the money to get dropped off. She was still going to let Savage know it was money on his head.

SAVAGE AND BEAUTY

9:30 P.M.

Savage pulled up to Dave and Buster's, him and Beauty smoked two fat ass J's in the car before they walked in. Soon as they got in Dave and Buster's, they went straight to eat. They ate wings and drunk some fruity shit Beauty ordered them. Beauty was tipsy, her eyes were low and chinky, giving her that foreign look. They played games all night, Beauty was hugging Savage, kissing him, and holding his hand all night.

She was having fun and starting to like Savage a lot. Dave's man, Pop, was in Dave and Buster's with his girl. He was shocked when he saw Beauty hugging and kissing another nigga. He was going to pull up on both of them, but he was on family time and ain't bring the dog with him. He told his girl to hold up, pulled out his phone, and took pictures of Beauty kissing Savage, sending them to Dave, thinking, *bitches ain't shit*.

"I had so much fun and I'm drunk, baby," Beauty told Savage, giggling as they hopped in the truck. "Can you fuck me right now?" Beauty asked Savage, pulling her dress up over her ass, sliding her thong down her legs, dropping them on the floor.

Savage sat his dog under the seat, pulled down his pants, and climbed between Beauty's thighs as she let her seat back. Beauty spread her legs as Savage slid in her deeper. Savage was digging his dick in and out her pussy, going in deep, grinding, pulling it to the tip, and sliding back in her deep, grinding. Beauty was loving it as she closed her eyes.

"Ohhh, Savage, I'm cummin', baby," she moaned, grabbing his back, pulling him in her deep. "Ahhh, Savage," she screamed, grinding on his dick as she came, feeling him cummin' in her. She let his back go, eyes still closed, body relaxed. Savage climbed out her pussy and climbed back in his seat, pulling up his pants. "Thank you, boo," Beauty told him, pulling her dress down, balling up in the seat, dosing off to sleep.

Savage grabbed his dog, sitting it on his lap. He grabbed some sheets and gas out the glove compartment and saw Beauty's phone and looked at it. It showed a picture of him, and Beauty hugged up, kissing. Under the picture, Dave wrote, "you fucking them young broke ass niggas, I got something for both y'all ass." Savage read it and deleted the text. Putting the phone back, he twisted up some gas, started the truck, and pulled off. *Oh, hell yeah, Dave ass going in the trunk, asap!*

SKY

11:50 P.M.

Sky slid up the stadium dolo, ice shining', designer down, and cookie on him. 15 bands on him, P90 Ruger on him, looking sweet. Soon as he stepped in the club, bitches thought he was a rapper with all that jewelry he had on. Sky hit the V.I.P dolo. Five bottles with the sparklers came to his table and two of the baddest bitches in the club with thongs stuffed all in their asses and pussy lips were sitting on his lap as he blew cookie in their faces. Sky drank two bottles of Ace, threw two bands in the air. He was high as shit, tipsy off the drinks and trying to fuck.

"What's up? I'm trying to fuck both of y'all. I got a band a piece," Sky told both the strippers, standing up feeling good. The strippers looked at each other, loving Sky's swag. They would've let him fuck for free, the money was just a plus.

"Hell, yeah we going. Let us go grab our shit, daddy," one of them said as they rushed off, ass clapping as they jogged to the locker room.

Sky grabbed the other bottle, taking a sip while waiting for the strippers to come back.

CHAPTER THIRTEEN

Freaky waited until the streets cleared when he felt everybody was sleep. He packed all his shit, guns, money, and clothes, and moved them to his other apartment Mrs. Jones got for him off the books. He watched the police and ambulance pick Mrs. Jones' body off the floor and tape her building off. All on his mind was killing anybody who knew where he lived. At 3:00a.m. his eyes were still on the news, his face still on each one.

He wasn't scared, just thinking how he was going to duck them cells. He had 200 bands, four guns, and a QP of gas. He started twisting up when Nook came to his mind. *Can I trust this nigga not to point the law in this direction?* He inhaled the smoke, letting his thoughts get the best of him. *I know Savage's lil ass solid, the lawyer, fuck it, I ain't taking no chances,* he said to himself, laying back on the couch fighting his demons.

SAVAGE

4:30 A.M.

Sky fucked both of the strippers all night off the perks. He left two bands on the table and left both of them in the hotel room sleep. He pulled up at Beauty's house, parking beside Beauty's Lex truck. The P90 Ruger went to his hip as he hopped out his truck. Soon as he walked in her apartment he smelled bacon, eggs, and cheese in the air. He looked and saw Beauty sitting on Savage lap, feeding him.

"What's up, slim?" Savage greeted.

"Same shit, switch-a-rooin' two bad bitches. Where the food at?" Sky asked, shutting, and locking the door behind him.

"Boy, you talking about bad bitches, pleaseee," Beauty told him, smiling, rolling her eyes. "And your plate in the microwave," she said, watching as he walked to the kitchen.

"Fire up, Moe, where the gas at?" Sky yelled from the kitchen as he heated up his food.

"Sky, you don't run shit in here. I'm not going to keep telling your ass that," Beauty told him seriously when her phone started ringing. She grabbed the phone, reading her text. Her whole mood changed as she read what Dave wrote.

"Dave's bitch ass on his way over here, Sky!" Beauty shrieked and ran to her room crying.

Sky got defensive off the brake. Hearing his sister crying, he sat his plate down. "Fuck up, what Dave purpin'?" He asked, ready to kill something as he walked to Beauty's room. Beauty had her door locked, telling Sky to leave her alone. "What the fucks up with her?" Sky asked Savage, walking back to the living room mad as shit.

"She got a text, but I know," Savage was about to tell Sky when they heard a knock on the door.

Sky snatched the P90 off his hip, strode to the door, and snatched it open. Dave searched Sky's face, recognizing the seriousness and the dog in his hand. He knew Sky was a killer, so he was nervous.

"Fuck is up with you and my sister?" Sky asked, looking in his eyes.

"Nothing, slim. Relationship shit, you know I'll never do nothing to your sister to hurt her, that's my heart," Dave told him, nervous, not knowing what Sky was thinking.

"Go holla at her, she crying. I be smoking niggas bout that shit, flat out," Sky told him, and Dave got the message as he nodded to Sky and walked to Beauty's room. He ain't look at Savage or greet him as he walked pass. Sky locked the door and sat next to Savage. Savage was twisting. "I'ma get that nigga, fuck it," Sky told Savage, sitting the P90 on the table as he grabbed the J from Savage.

"I read a text the nigga wrote Beauty. He wrote Beauty

that he saw a picture of us last night in Dave and Buster's, kissing. I don't know how the nigga got it but Beauty went to sleep. I grabbed her phone and saw he wrote some slick shit like; he got something for the both of us," Savage told him, grabbing the J.

"Yeah, we on his ass. And you looking through Beauty's phone while she sleep and shit, fuck is up with your pervert ass, nigga," Sky joked, laughing when he saw Dave and Beauty walking out the room.

"We'll be back," Beauty notified them, giving them a weak smile.

"I got another joint for you to pull up later, Sky," Dave said, phone by his ear like he was talking but he was taking pictures of Sky and Savage the whole time as him and Beauty walked out the apartment.

"Yeah, I'm flushing the nigga," Sky declared, laying back on the couch, blowing gas in the air.

DETECTIVE GRAM AND ROB

11:50 A.M.

Detective Gram had come back from Atlanta talking to Tiana. They believed what she told them about Freaky. That was another murder he was going to be charged with. They still hadn't received an address or a phone call about his whereabouts. They put him on *America's Most Wanted*, feeling he was out of the city. They did all the paperwork on Freaky, Savage, and Sky.

Lil D was in a witness protection program, letting them know everything about Gucci and why he was beefing with Sky. Detective Rob put a warrant out for Savage's arrest for killing Pee-Wee. They wanted to get Savage to tell on Freaky and get him to tell them Freaky's whereabouts. They had police officers watching his aunt's house 24/7. They were waiting one more week, knowing Savage wouldn't show up for court.

Detective Gram and Rob found out Gucci was shot up and that his girl was killed in her apartment. They had an idea who did it but went and paid him a visit. When the detectives walked in Gucci's hospital room, he was in a fucked-up way. He was talking and breathing on his own but was on a shit and piss bag. Gucci got shot 18 times. Luckily, the car slowed some of the bullets down, it was the only reason he was still alive. He'd died on the operating table three times. Gucci had to get his lung taking out. He still had a long road to recovery.

"Mr. Johnson," Detective Rob greeted, walking up to his bed as Detective Gram walked around the room and took a seat right in front of Gucci's bed. "Shot 18 times, caught with a mac 11, and 200 thousand dollars in cash. You're already a convicted felon, so you already know you going to the Feds. Your girlfriend Me-Me was found in her apartment dead with a gunshot wound to the back of her head. I know about your beef with Sky and him killing your cousin," Detective Rob said, peering in Gucci's face.

"Damn, Me-Me got killed," Gucci said to himself. *Damn, shit bad.*

"I believe Sky and Savage shot you up right after they killed Shooter, am I right?" Detective Rob asked. Gucci didn't reply but was glad they ain't know he had killed Shooter. "I know you might not want to talk right now, so I'ma leave my card on the table. Help me, help you," Detective Rob stated, sitting his card on the table beside his bed.

"Think about it," Gram added as they walked out the room.

Fuck I look like telling, they got me fucked up, Gucci said to himself, looking at the card, shaking his head.

DAVE

Right after Dave dropped Beauty off, he was still upset because Beauty told him they needed a break. He asked was it because of Savage and she told him, "yeah." His self-esteem was bruised. *This broke ass young nigga ain't got shit on me.* He was going off emotions when he called Tyson, telling him he had some important shit to holla at him about. Dave met Tyson in Exits parking lot. Soon as Dave hopped in Tyson's car, Tyson greeted him, dapping Dave up.

"What's up, slim?" He asked, watching Dave going through his phone.

"That's Savage and that's Sky," Dave told him, pointing to the pictures on his phone.

"Shit!" Tyson cussed, laughing. *That's the same two muthafuckas that robbed me.* "This good, slim," Tyson told him, telling Dave to send the pictures to his phone.

"I got both of them meeting me today," Dave told him, looking at Tyson, letting him know he was going to set the play. "Do that asap, I got you," Dave said, shaking Tyson's hand. *Fuck Savage and Sky*, Dave was thinking as Tyson sent the pictures to Tone and dialed Keem's number. It was a work call.

CHAPTER FOURTEEN

$\mathcal{P}$am had been having morning sickness for the last week, waking up, throwing up, feeling tired and sluggish. Her father took her to the doctor and found out she was six weeks pregnant. He was in a rage, fucked up that someone got his 14-year-old daughter pregnant. Pam's father, Karl Ellis, was a killer back in the day. He did 20 years straight on a hitman for hire charge.

He came home and saw life in a different. Too much telling, nigga wasn't respecting the game. He said fuck the streets, got a job, and was raising his daughter. Once a killer, *always* a killer. So, once he questioned Pam about the father, she didn't want to tell him. And with Freaky's face all over the news for murder and rape, she definitely didn't want him to know. Karl kept pressing until Pam put her head down, tears rolling down her cheeks, and said Freaky's name.

BUBBLES

1:50 P.M.

Tone had to do some running around for the last two days. Bubbles hit the club and Star was throwing shade, fake smiles and hey's. Bubbles saw right through that shit. Bubbles and her buddy, Whitegirl, partied all night, getting that money. They ran into some niggas from New York throwing cash and wanting to have fun. Bubbles and Whitegirl drugged them, got everything, and made their escape. They were in the mall the next day shopping. Bubbles was buying Savage some Dior shoes and an outfit when her phone chimed with a text message.

"This nigga on a bitch line," Bubbles told Whitegirl, putting the clothes on the counter when she saw the text showing Sky and Savage. The text was asking if she knew them. Bubbles' heart dropped in her chest as she texted back: *I never saw them before*.

Whitegirl saw the look and asked was she okay; she was concerned. Bubbles told her she was cool and started dialing Savage's number, telling the clerk and Whitegirl she'd be right back, walking out of Nordstrom as the phone rang.

"Right after we pull the move, we grab Dave's bitch ass next," Sky told Savage as he pulled off the highway, headed out Forestville.

"You already know what's up," Savage said, watching the

mirrors as he grabbed his phone, hearing it ring. He saw it was Bubbles and answered. "What's up, boo?"

"Tone and Tyson got pictures of you and Sky," Bubbles said in a rush, cutting Savage off. "I heard it's money on yours and Freaky's heads, please be careful. Two more days, boo, please be careful. I love you, Savage," Bubbles told him, hanging up when she saw Whitegirl walking out the store to check on her.

"You know a Tone and Tyson?" Savage asked Sky as he pulled up Forestville, parking by McDonalds.

"Tone and Tyson," he said, thinking. "Naw, why, what's up?" Sky asked, concerned.

"Bubbles just hit me saying the nigga got pictures of us and got money on our heads."

"Kill!" Sky yelled, grinning. "Fuck that nigga, he could get flushed just like anybody else, but best believe I'ma do my research," Sky said, watching Dave drive into the parking lot.

Dave pulled beside their truck, parked, and hopped out, getting into Sky's car, sitting in the backseat. Savage turned in his seat, watching him, hand around the trigger. Savage hated niggas sitting behind him and he didn't trust Dave period.

"Look, slim, the nigga Money got it loaded. I want y'all to do the same thing. I got the same 30 for y'all, just give me the work. I'ma hit y'all soon as it's time," Dave said, looking at Sky. He glanced at Savage, thinking, *broke ass nigga.*

"Bet, hit me," Sky told him, nodding as he hopped out the truck.

Dave and Savage ain't say nothing to each other. Dave nodded to Keem on the lows as he hopped out his car. *Please kill both them bitch ass niggas*, Dave said to himself, pulling out the parking lot. Keem and his right-hand man Lil E from 37th was in a chipped up Intrepid, Drakos in the car, watching. Tyson gave Keem 50 to flush them niggas, so Keem was on a mission. He watched the truck drive off and waited ten seconds before pulling off behind them.

"What you gon' do bout the court shit?" Savage asked as they hit the highway back to the city.

"Fuck them peoples, they got to catch me. I'm bouta stop playing Beauty's joint, I know that's the first spot they going to hit. That's why a nigga need a big lick. At least 300, a nigga could lamp a lil bit. Go fuck with your man Stuntman in Miami," Sky told him, stopping at the light across the street from the bowling alley.

Savage glanced in the mirror seeing an Intrepid with two young niggas in it, speeding up on Sky's side of the door. "Get down!" Savage yelled, grabbing Sky, pushing them flat down under the passenger seat.

Savage was opening his door, climbing out when shots went off. Keem pulled right up, him and Lil E hopped out and got to clicking. **Blocka, Blocka, Blocka, Blocka, Blocka, Blocka!** People were running and cars were running red lights trying to get away, as Keem and Lil E Swiss-cheesed the truck. Emptying their clips, they hopped back in the Intrepid, hauling ass. Keem said, "if a nigga survived that, they were God," as he did the dash up the highway.

TYSON

6:50 P.M.

Tyson walked in Exits, showing all the strippers and workers the pictures of Savage and Sky. Even though he knew they were getting killed today, he was thinking just in case the hit ain't go right, he wanted to know their resume. China saw the picture and remembered Savage from fingering Bubbles and from the day Tyson was robbed. *I'ma stick a lil closer to this bitch Bubbles. I smell some fishy shit going on.*

Star saw the picture and was upset. She told herself next time she saw Bubbles, she was going to let her know to warn Savage. She didn't want nothing to happen to him.

CHAPTER FIFTEEN

Freaky's lawyer, Brian McDaniels, had been fighting with his demons. Viewing Freaky's face on the news, deliberating, *what if that was my family? I got to let the police know where he is staying,* Brian thought, cutting off the T.V., getting in his bed, and telling himself he was getting in touch with the police personally. *Freaky got to go to jail for these crimes.*

FREAKY

12:01 A.M.

Freaky watched how the streets moved, who stayed out late, what time people went to work, everybody's routine. At 12:01a.m. Freaky left out his apartment, all-black on, hood on his head, and jogged out the backdoor, hopping in his Honda. Watching his surroundings, he pulled out the parking lot. He had some loose ends to handle.

DAVE

4:00 A.M.

Dave was in the house all day watching the news, praying Tyson handled the situation with Savage and Sky because he already knew if they didn't get flushed, they were going to be hipped that he pulled the play. He was nervous as shit. Smoking, drinking, and pacing all night. Dave even called Beauty a couple times to check her temperature on Sky and Savage. She didn't sound worried like something was wrong, so that really had him on edge.

He didn't catch the news about the shooting until 3:59 in the morning. The news broadcasted a shooting, where the police found over 50 shell casings at the scene. The reporter also alerted that witnesses saw two men fleeing the scene after the shooting. Police were looking for the suspects and the owner of the Audi truck. After hearing the end of the news report, Dave got up off the couch in a hurry. He ran to his room, packing all his shit.

"I got to get the fuck gone, asap!" He grumbled out loud, putting all his money and jewelry in his bag. Dave peeked out the window, nervously peeping around, drumming in his chest.

He was scared. *Fuck, I shouldn't of did that shit!* Shaking as he left the apartment, he stopped at the hallway building door. Looking out, it was still dark, street lights on. He didn't see any movement as he left the apartment, opened the door, and ran to his car.

Savage and Sky had been parked beside Dave's 650 since 10:00p.m. after the attempt on their lives. Beauty picked them up from Suitland Apartments. Soon as they got to her house, they hopped out the car and hopped straight in Savage's truck and pulled off. All that was on their minds was killing Dave. They were taking turns sleeping, keeping eyes on Dave's apartment.

They knew he was home because they saw lights on, movement, and the 650 parked. They were going to wait him out until he showed his face, even if it took months. Sky was still awake, texting the stripper bitch he met at the club the other night. Her name was Raven, and she was on Sky's heels. She really wanted to fuck with him, plus she did her research and found out he was a sho 'nuff nigga and that boosted it even more.

Sky texted her, telling her he was tryna fuck. He glanced up, seeing Dave speed-walking out the building. Sky dropped his phone, shaking Savage awake, grabbing his Ruger as he jumped out the car. Dave saw Sky, turned, and sprinted up the parking lot.

Boom! Boom! Boom! Boom! Boom!
Sky pulled the trigger, chasing Dave up the parking lot.

"Ahhh," Dave yelled, running as fast as he could. He felt a bullet rip through his shoulder but kept running, adrenaline rushing. He shook it off, not wanting to get smoked as he ducked, bullets flying by his head.

He was running, cutting through buildings, trying to get away.

Boom! Boom! Click-Clack.

Sky decocked as he watched Dave cut through a building, getting away.

"Bitch ass nigga!" Sky screamed, as Savage pulled up beside him. Sky hopped in the truck as the lights in the apartments started cutting on. "Bitch ass nigga got away, I'ma catch his ass," Sky told Savage as Savage did the dash out the parking lot.

Dave ran up to the Amazon girl, Danny's house, arm leaking, breathing hard, and thanking God he got away as Danny called the ambulance for him.

BRIAN MCDANIELS

6:30AM

Brian McDaniels pulled up to his office at 6:31a.m. He came early so he could get in touch with the police chief himself, to let him know everything he knew about Freaky. He hopped out his car, trotted to his office, and saw a homeless man with all-black on, sleeping on his steps with a hood over his head. Brian walked up and shook him awake.

"You got to move," he told the homeless man and froze in shock when Freaky lifted his head, Glock in his hand.

Boom! The gun went off, hitting Brian in the head. Freaky shot him again and broke to his car. *I'm killing all loose ends, fuck that!*

CHAPTER SIXTEEN

Two days later, August 12th, 2020, at 6:50a.m. Tone met up with Tyson at the pickup spot. He picked up 800 thousand for the reup, he gave Tyson 30 bricks of heroin, 95% raw, dapped him up, and they made small talk and went about their business. Tone usually would go put the money in the stash first then he'd make plans for other things. Tone had just ducked a conspiracy charge. He knew he was being watched and even though he had businesses and could fight it, he knew if he got pulled over and the police found 800 bands, they would open another case on him.

He went against his own better judgement and went to Bubbles' complex to pick her up. Bubbles had been texting him all morning, wanting to spend the day with him. Tone pulled up to Bubbles' house and texted he was out front. Bubbles came out her building five minutes later, dreads in a ponytail hanging to her ass. She had on some lil ass boy shorts that stopped at the top of her thighs.

Her legs were lotioned, glowing. She had on some open toe sandals, feet done, nails done, and lip gloss on her lips. Her titties were sitting up in her shirt, Bubbles was looking good as shit. Tone grabbed his dick as he watched her sexy ass walking to his truck, smiling.

"Hey, daddy… how are you?" she greeted, hopping in the car. She leaned over the seat, kissing Tone's lips.

"I'm cool. Good morning, beautiful," Tone told her, grinning as he pulled out the parking lot.

DAVE

12:50 P.M.

After Dave got patched up from the shooting, he was scared to go home. Dave called Tyson to pick him up from the hospital.

"Fuck happened to you?" Tyson asked, looking at Dave's arm in a sling.

"The niggas Sky and Savage ain't dead. They were in front of my house waiting on me," he told Tyson as he pulled off. "I'm lucky to be alive right now. I got the money; I need a couple more joints. I'ma give you the nigga Sky's sister's address where they be at. I'ma slide out of town for a second," Dave told Tyson, giving him the address and a picture of Beauty and what type of car, she drove as they went to pick up the money and work. "Fuck all them, Beauty picked the wrong nigga," Dave said to himself.

SAVAGE AND SKY

9:20 P.M.

"Savageeee, I fucking love youuuu," Dawn screamed, legs bent by her head. Savage was slow stroking his dick in her stomach. "Oohhh my Savage," she moaned as Savage sped up, pounding her pussy. His whole mid-section was wet from Dawn's pussy juice. Savage was loving it, creaming all over his dick, pussy getting wetter each time she came. "Nut in this pussy, daddy. I want it in this pussy!" Dawn screamed, closing her eyes, cumming on Savage, feeling it in her stomach as he came deep in her pussy.

She wrapped her legs around his waist, pulling him deeper as she kissed all over his face. Sky was in the living room sleep. He was drained from being up all night, two days straight, searching and trying to kill Dave's scary ass. Sky blew a 7th of some good gas, ate 20-piece nuggets, two double cheese burgers, and fell asleep on the couch, exhausted.

"I'm pregnant, Savage," Dawn whispered in his ear as he rolled on his side.

"Oh, yeah?" Savage replied through slit eyes, not really listening to her.

"Yeah, and it's *yours*," Dawn told him, looking in his face.

"Oh, yeah," Savage told her again and dosed off to sleep.

Dawn just looked at him smiling. "I'm in love with you, lil boy," she said out loud, kissing him on the lips. She put the cover over both of them, her ass on his dick. She put his arm around her and dosed off to sleep.

BUBBLES

11:30 P.M.

"Throw that ass in a circle," Bubbles sang as she stood in Tone's room in just a red thong, clapping her ass for him. Tone was tipsy off a bottle of Ace him and Bubbles drank. Tone stood up, grabbing Bubbles by the waist.

FREAKY

1:15AM

"Nook, what's up, Slim?" Freaky greeted, looking out the blinds of his apartment, drako in his hand, watching to see any fucked-up movement. He'd already made up in his mind that he was dying before the law caught him and took him to jail. Fuck that!

"Damn, Slim, your face all over the news everyday all day. Fuck is up?" Nook asked, sitting on the couch, watching the

T.V. in his aunt's house. After that shit Savage and Sky did, spanking Murder and them simp, Nook moved asap and never went back up simp.

"You know how shit be. Fuck all that though, I need you to hold something for me, slim. Where you staying? I be moving late. When the streets clear up, I need you," Freaky told him.

"I got you, Slim. Me and Jammy up my Aunt Peaches' joint. I been looking for a lick so I can move asap."

Freaky's dick got hard thinking about Nook's lil sister's good lil pussy. "I'ma hit you when I pull up. She still live up E St., right?" Freaky asked, grabbing his dick, thinking about fucking Jammy again.

"Yeah, same spot. Just hit me, I got you," Nook told him, hanging up. *This nigga Freaky outta control.*

BUBBLES

3:30 A.M.

Bubbles and Tone drunk four bottles of Ace and fucked like rabbits. Bubbles sucked Tone to sleep and swallowed everything. Bubbles laid beside him, faking like she was sleep until she heard him snoring. Bubbles climbed out the bed, grabbing her phone. Eyes still on Tone, she made sure he was still sleep as she tip-toed out the room. Bubbles texted Savage Tone's address as she speed-walked down the steps and unlocked the front door.

She texted Savage that the front door was open. She jogged back to Tone's room, and he was still sleeping, snoring. Bubbles deleted the text and put the phone on the floor. She threw on a shirt, climbed back on the bed, and laid her head on Tone's chest, acting like she was sleeping.

KEEM AND LIL E

3:50 A.M.

Keem and Lil E pulled up in front of Beauty's house looking at her picture on Lil E's phone. Lil E scanned the parking lot, seeing two police cruisers sitting two buildings down.

"The law, Slim, pull off," Lil E told Keem, putting his 45 under his thigh, watching to see if they pulled behind them.

"We a get her," Keem said, riding out the parking lot.

TONE

4:40 A.M.

Tone was in a deep sleep, snoring hard when he felt something metal tapping his face. Tone woke up starring down the barrel of a big ass 45th. He looked around. *This shit got to be a dream.* He saw Bubbles laid out on the floor, gun to her head and tears streaming down her face.

"Where the shit at, *everything*?" Savage asked him. You could hear in his voice that this shit was serious.

Tone looked around then in Savage's eyes. *This that nigga Savage!* "It's two duffel bags in the backyard, in the dog house. I know the rules of the game, you caught me lackin', it's yours, Slim," Tone said in a calm voice, mad as shit at himself for moving so sloppy, praying he lived to see another day.

Savage looked at Sky. "Bitch don't move or I promise I'ma smoke your ass," Savage told Bubbles, 45th still pointed in Tone's face. Sky ran out the room to get the money. "Bitch ass old niggas putting money on my head. Look at this wild nigga," Savage said to himself, trigger finger itching.

Sky ran back in the room with two duffle bags in his hands. "We loaded, Moe," Sky told Savage.

Savage pulled the trigger.

Boom!

"Ahhh," Tone yelled as the first bullet grazed his head. He ducked, trying to curl up.

Boom! Boom! Boom!

Bullets hit Tone all in his body. Blood poured out of his body, all on the sheets as Tone struggled for his breath. Bubbles was in shock, watching Tone fight for his life as Sky and Savage ran out the room. "Helllppp," Tone struggled to say, it was getting harder to breathe.

Bubbles grabbed her phone, calling 911 as she watched

Tone's chest stop rising. His eyes were closed as blood poured out his body.

FREAKY

4:41 A.M.

At 4:41a.m. Freaky pulled up 187 D and circled the block four times before he parked. He didn't call Nook before he came. He didn't know why but he didn't trust him at all after all that D-Boy shit when Nook cuffed that money. He was a snake so he felt like if you did some snake shit once, you'd do it again because he would. Freaky hopped out the Honda, all-black on, hood on his head, hand around the 18 in his hoodie pocket, speed walking to Nook's building.

Freaky looked out the building door, making sure no one was following him. He walked to Nook's apartment and knocked. Nook tried to wait on Freaky to call, but when he didn't call by 2:00a.m. Nook dosed off to sleep. Nook's aunt was 56 years old. She was a 9 to 5 worker and went to sleep every day at 10:00p.m., closing her door.

Jammy walked out the kitchen to get something to drink when she heard a knock. She was still tired, rubbing her eyes as she walked down the hallway. She opened the door and was looking in Freaky's face.

"What's up?" Freaky greeted, stepping in the house, backing her against the wall as he locked the door behind him.

"Jammy," he whispered in her ear as he ran his hands down her body. Jammy's pussy was dripping wet as Freaky stripped her pajama pants to her ankles. He pulled down her panties, rubbing his fingers up and down her slit, rubbing her phat clit. "Ohhh," she moaned as Freaky laid her down on the hallway floor, stripped her pants and panties completely off, put his 18 on the floor as he spread her legs and pulled out his dick, sliding in and out of her at a fast pace.

"Ahhh... Ohhh... Freaky..." she screamed, cumming on his dick, opening her legs wider, and letting him get as deep as he wanted. Nook heard moaning as he woke up. He heard it again. *I know Jammy ain't in here fucking.* "Ima fuck her stupid ass up," he said, getting up and creeping up to the moaning.

"Ohh shit! I'm cumming again," Jammy screamed. Freaky slid deep in her, nutting big, filling coming from his balls.

"Freaky, fuck is you doing?" Nook yelled in shock, walking up to Freaky. Freaky grabbed the 18 off the floor, pointing it at Nook. Nook stopped in his tracks. Freaky grinned while pulling up his pants. Jammy grabbed her pants, hurriedly putting them on, knowing she fucked up.

"Aye Nook, fuck was you about to do?" Freaky asked, putting his foot on Jammy's back as she tried to get up. "Don't move," he told her, glaring at Nook's gun still pointed at him as he dropped his pants.

"Fuck is you doing, Moe?" Nook asked while watching Freaky grab Jammy by her hair.

"Suck my dick… suck it or I'ma kill you." He told her, still staring at Nook. Jammy started crying as she grabbed his dick, inserting it in her mouth. Freaky gawked at Nook grinning. Nook was looking at Freaky, thinking, *this nigga lunching.*

"Fuck is this about, Slim? That's my folks… come on, Slim." Nook pleaded while watching his sister sucking Freaky's dick.

"You snaked me for 5 bands with that D-boy shit, wild nigga," Freaky told him and pulled the trigger.

Pow!

The bullet hit Nook in his chest, and Jammy took Freaky's dick out her mouth in a panic and tried to crawl away.

Pow!

Freaky pulled the trigger, shooting Jammy in her back.

"Ahhh…" she cried, lying flat on the floor. Freaky walked up to her and pulled the trigger again.

Pow!

Shooting Jammy in the back of her head. Nook was holding his chest, eyes big from fear, trying to catch his breath as Freaky walked up to him.

"Fuck you," Freaky told him and shot Nook in his face.

"What the fuck is going on out there, Nook, Jammy?" Aunt Peaches yelled from her bed nervously after hearing gunshots.

"Nook?" She called again and grabbed her phone, calling

911 as she fearfully staggered to her bedroom door thinking the worst.

"This is 9-1-1, how can I help you?" the operator asked as Peaches opened her room door.

Pow!

Freaky pulled the trigger, shooting Aunt Peaches in her face, then turning and fleeing out the apartment before the body dropped.

Neighbors came out their apartments to investigate the shooting, some people saw Freaky fleeing out the building. The neighbors ran to Aunt Peaches' apartment and froze at the sight of all that blood all over the floor, it was a *massacre*. Nook was still alive, bloody, eyeing the neighbors. "Helpppp," he tried to say, choking on his own blood. One of the neighbors ran to Nook, holding him, talking to him, trying to keep him alive. Other neighbors called the police, shaking their heads, viewing Jammy's dead body, thinking, *whoever did this is a fucking savage!*

Aunt Peaches died with the phone beside her. All you heard was the operator asking, "What's going on?"

BUBBLES

Bubbles stayed with Tone's body until the police and ambulance came. Bubbles rode with Tone's body to the hospital and got questioned for hours by the police about what happened. When Tyson and Big Mike showed up Bubbles was still crying, bloody, playing the part as Tyson questioned her thoroughly. Big Mike talked to the doctors, and they informed them that Tone was on the operation table fighting for his life. Tone was shot 13 times, and it was 90% chance he wasn't going to make it. Tyson was fucked up hearing this. Big Mike just prayed as they watched Bubbles leave. She was bloody, eyes red, physically, and mentally drained.

"You think that bitch set Tone up?" Tyson asked Big Mike, hoping he say *yeah* so, he could kill somebody, he was hurting.

"I don't think so, but I've seen a lot… if she did, she's a hell of an actor, flat out." Big Mike told him, letting his mind wonder.

Bubbles took an Uber home, watching everything, making sure she wasn't being followed. She got out the Uber and trekked up the block, walking back to her building when she was sure no one was following her. When she wandered in her apartment, she seen Savage and Sky sitting on the floor smoking. It was stacks of money all over the floor. Savage saw how drained and tired Bubbles looked. He handed Sky the J and walked up and grabbed Bubbles' hand. Sky nodded to Bubbles as Savage lead her to the bathroom, he cut on the shower as he took Bubbles' clothes off.

"We counted 400 bands, it's still more cash to go." Savage told her as he took off his clothes, getting in the shower with her. He washed her body, watching the blood flow down the drain. He kissed her lips and bent her over, Bubbles put her hands on the side of the tub. Savage slid in her.

"I love you, Bubbles," Savage told her, speeding up his stroke as the water hit their backs.

"Ohhh Savage, I love youuuu," she cried as Savage punished Bubbles' pussy, nutting all in her. They washed up again, he dried her off, put a towel around her, and escorted her to the room. Bubbles got into bed, pulling up the covers, and Savage kissed her on the lips.

"I love you, lil boy," she told him and dosed off to sleep. Savage put on a t-shirt, some shorts, socks, and grabbed his mini 5th and walked back to the living room.

"Bout time… you got me counting all this shit my myself, we at 500 bands, get to work, wild ass nigga." Sky told Savage, handing him the J, laughing as they counted up.

BEAUTY

6:50 A.M.

Beauty woke up at 6:50a.m. to banging on her door. "What, who the fuck is that?" Beauty yelled, putting on a pair of sweatpants and a t-shirt as she walked to her front door, looking out the peephole, seeing police officers.

Beauty opened the door. "We're here for your brother, here is the warrant to look around," an officer told her, handing

Beauty the warrant, enforcing his way in the house looking for Sky.

Beauty was steaming, watching as officers check each room not finding Sky. "Your brother has an outstanding warrant out for his arrest." Beauty just looked at the officer, really not listening, she was waiting for them to leave so she could call and cuss Sky's ass out. Soon as the Marshalls left, she shut and locked her door, grabbing her phone pacing and calling Sky.

"Who the fuck you keep textin' and shit? Ain't you tied, Moe?" Savage asked, sitting the last stack on the floor, laying back, and looking at Sky.

"Lil stripper bitch name Raven, bad lil bitch too. I fucked her and her buddy Megan, but I been texting back and forth with Raven, 'that's my lil bitch'." Sky told 'em, grinning when his phone started ringing. "Beauty," Sky mouthed as Savage had answered.

"First, don't bring your ass back to the house, I'm taking your ass off the lease today… got the police running in here lookin' for your big head ass. Second, I need some money and where is Savage?" she demanded, taking a seat on the couch.

"I got 50 bands for you so all that yelling and shit, slow down before you don't get shit," Sky was about to tell Beauty that Savage was right here until he saw Bubbles walk in the living room laying on Savage lap. "He went up to his folks' house… I'ma get with him later doe."

"Alright but what's up with the money?" she asked.

"I'ma meet up with you later, love you sis," he told her.

"Love you too… stay out of trouble and don't come here, I know the police watching the house." Beauty told him and hung up as she walked to her room. *It's too early to be up.*

"It's 800 bands, 2 short of a M," Savage told Bubbles, grabbing her ass.

"Damn!" she screeched, smiling, thinking about her hair salon she wanted to open. "So, what's my cut?" She asked, looking at all them stacks sitting all over the floor.

"You get 300, it was your play, me and Sky split 250 apiece," he said.

"You lucky we fuck with you," Sky said, smiling, watching as Bubbles got up and grabbed stacks.

She looked at Sky. "Boy, I earned this shit. I'm getting my shop!" she screamed. Savage just watched because he was tired as shit.

NOOK

9:50 A.M.

Nook got shot in the chest and his face, both bullets went in and out. He was real bloody, but the wounds weren't life threatening. He was cool but still had a couple more days to go in the hospital. Nook still couldn't come to grips with his aunt and lil sister being killed. He blamed his self but never in a million years did he think Freaky would do something like that. He said to himself, tears falling down his cheeks.

"Mr. Wood," Detective Rob greeted as him and his partner Detective Gram walked in his room. Nook wiped tears from his face. Detective Rob and Gram just found out the semen that was in Jammy's body belonged to Freaky. They did their research and found out Nook and Freaky had been friends for years. The detectives were praying Nook talked and gave them the whereabouts on Freaky. They need that animal off the streets or dead.

Nook looked at the detectives, tears rolling down his face. "Fuck Freaky and everybody he love. Freaky killed my family! I know his address where he lives, I know about Savage and Sky killing them dudes up Simple City after Freaky got shot and I'm willing to testify, fuck them niggas!"

CHAPTER SEVENTEEN

Sky Next Day

Sky bought himself a 2017 smoke gray Range Sport from Big Mike for $50,000. Sky pulled up 22nd parking, he hopped out Gucci down, 50 bands worth of jewelry on his neck, ears, wrist, and a Glock 22 with the 36 in it on his hip. Sky grabbed his bookbag off the backseat, put it on his back, and walked in the courts. Niggas were standing in front of the building, watching him, wondering who the fuck he was. Bitches were necking, seeing a new face, pussy jumping thinking he up. Sky felt eyes on him but he wasn't worried as he made his way to building 650. It was two niggas and three bitches sitting on the building steps smoking, the bitches were looking at Sky with lust in their eyes.

"What's up, Slim?" one of the dudes said.

"What's up?" Sky asked, looking at the dude that spoke. The dude that spoke was watching, hand by his waist.

"I'm Squirrel. This my man Frank Jones." He pointed to the dude whose hand went to his hip.

"I'm Sky, slim. I'ma be staying around here a lil bit," Sky said, dapping them up.

"Bet, if you looking for some hoes, fuck with me." Frank Jones said as Sky walked in the building. Two of the girls were Jones' and Squirrel's girls, the other one's name was DD, she was just there hoovering up the weed. Jones' and Squirrel's girls were twins, named Tia and Tamia, all three of them was thinking the same thing. They wanted to see what that dick do.

Sky walked to apartment 4. Hearing music playing, he knocked with his hand on the Glock, watching the hallway door. He saw the look in them bitches' eyes, plus he knew he was a lick. He wasn't doing no lackin'. The door opened, and Raven was standing there in a tank top and boy shorts looking good, flat out. Raven was in love with Sky. She stripped so she been around all type of boss niggas. She was bad, 5'3", 120 pounds, brown skin, nice sexy body, plump ass, titties, and feet a torch. She had them lips that had niggas going crazy, that Meagan Good look. Her lil ass was phat. She didn't know what it was, but she couldn't get enough of Sky.

"Bitch, who is that?" Megan yelled, walking to the door in a t-shirt and a pair of leggings, her phat ass looking just like the rap bitch Doja Cat, thick like her and everything.

"Skyyy," Megan sung as she watched Raven jump on him, wrapping her leg around his waist, kissing his lips.

"Twist up. I'm up here," Sky told both of them, palming Raven's plump ass cheeks, as he carried her to the living room.

SAVAGE

1:50 P.M.

Savage dropped 80 bands on a 2015 Ferrari Coupe sky blue joint. Big Mike asked Savage where he got all the money from.

"Off the land," Savage told him, dapping him up as he pulled off the lot, Moneybagg Yo blasting out the speakers. Savage pulled up Trinidad. When he pulled up 16th in front of building 1027, Po and Bishop were posted in front the building watching. Savage hopped out the Ferrari dressed Versace down. Versace shades on his face, "Savage Shit" chain around his neck, P90 with the beam and 36 in it on him looking sweet. Moneybagg Yo was still blasting out the speakers as he walked up to Po.

"You purpin'." Po smiled as he dapped Savage up.

Savage dapped Bishop up.

"What's up, Moe. Where them licks at?" Bishop asked while looking Savage up and down.

"Wild nigga, I'm a lick I.F.L., stupid nigga," Savage told

him and turned his attention back to Po. Savage ain't fuck with Bishop period. Only reason he spoke was off the strength of Po.

"I see you, Slim," Po said as a junkie walked up, he served him, and told Savage he needed to holla at him about something.

"Come on," Savage told Po as he walked to the car, hopping in. Po hopped in too and Savage pulled off. Bishop was watching him, hate in his eyes. Savage pulled by the Rec and parked, taking some gas and sheets out his pockets and twisting up.

"I been fuckin' with this Maryland nigga, and I been spending 60 bands each time every 3 days. The other day, he raised the price on me, and the coke was trash… shit ain't lock up good. I had to beat the shit out the pots." Po laughed and grabbed the jay from Savage.

"I'ma put in an order tonight for 5, tell 'em throw me 4, give me the bricks. I'ma give you 50 bands," Po said, looking in Savage's eyes.

"50?" Savage asked. "I got you," he told Po, cutting up the music as they got high.

BUBBLES

Bubbles first stop was the car lot. She traded in her Lex truck and put an extra 40 thousand and got her an all cocaine white on white Maybach Coupe. Bubbles got in touch with a realtor and asked about a couple of condos that were for sale in the Woodbridge, Virginia area. She met up with a realtor named Mrs. Jessica who showed her a nice two-bedroom condo with washer and dryer included. Bubbles loved it and loved the area; it was nice and quiet.

"How much is the asking price?" Bubbles asked.

"It's $150,000 to own," Mrs. Jessica stated.

"I got $100,000 now cash and $5000 for you if you could make the paperwork look good. I'll pay the other $50,000 monthly on a year lease to make it look good," Bubbles told her, looking in Mrs. Jessica eyes.

Mrs. Jessica was weighing her options and asked, "Do you have the money now?"

"Yes, right now. I would like to sign and move in today," Bubbles told her.

"You got a deal." Mrs. Jessica shook Bubble's hand.

Next stop for Bubbles was the strip club. She met up with Tyson and told him she was done dancing. After what happened to Tone, she couldn't do it anymore. Tyson understood and tried to give her some going away money, but she declined and walked from the club without looking back. Bubbles stopped to eat with her friend Whitegirl, letting her know her goals and that she wanted Whitegirl to manage the salon for her when it opened.

SKY

2:51 P.M.

Give her back shots till her back hurt, counting throwing the bands to my hands hurt, 21 Savage blasted out the speakers.

"Yess…. Shit, I'm coming again." Raven yelled as she bounced up and down, sliding and grinding, cumming all over Sky's dick. Sky picked her up, laying her on the couch. He stood up ass naked except his Cristian Louis, his watch, and chain. Raven sat up on the couch ass naked, pussy creamy, grabbing the J and firing it up.

Megan was standing at the window, looking out, bouncing her ass to the music. "Who's that?" Sky asked, leaning over Megan's shoulder, putting his dick on Megan's ass, and looking out the window as she bounced her soft ass up and down his dick.

"That's Squirrel and Frank Jones," she said, pointing to the two brown skin dudes sitting on the steps with two bitches sitting on their laps.

"They run shit around here. Them two dirty ass bitches are sisters. Tia and Tamia. Them bitches will do anything." She rolled her eyes, lifting his dick up with her ass, dropping it, grinding, she was horny. Sky reached his hand around her, putting his hand in her leggings, rubbing her pussy, pumping a finger in and out of her pussy slowly.

"The other three dude's names are Rob, Sam, and Drake

dirty ass. Rob and Sam be getting a lil cash, robbing," Megan moaned as she rotated her pussy on his fingers, rotating her ass on his dick. Sky took his finger out her pants, seeing pussy juice dripping off them.

"The black ass dirty nigga. He be robbing and shit. Him and his lil team, but for real, them niggas broke and snakes, I hate their ass." Megan told him as Sky pulled her leggings down to her ankles, he pulled her soaking wet thong down her thighs and bent her over the window sill. He rubbed his dick up and down her hot, moist slit before sliding inside of her, spreading her ass cheeks, watching his dick slip in and out her pussy.

"Daddy's home," he whispered in Megan's ear.

"Shittt," Raven moaned, finger fucking herself, watching Sky fuck Megan!

ANT

12:01 A.M.

Ant was from Homer Ave by Suitland High School. He was plugged. His father was a nigga named Big Jon, who was a coke man and made sure his son touched 20 bricks a month or better for 17 a joint. Ant had Maryland on lock. Both him and his right-hand man D.J. were winning.

Ant had Po throw a bitch they both was fucking. He started off charging Po 60 for two joints. Po was running through that shit like water. They had a good relationship until Ant started catching feelings for the bitch and wanted her to stop fucking with Po. The bitch told Ant *no,* flat out, and cut him off. Ant saw her two weeks later in the passenger seat of Po's 550, and got so mad, he started taxing Po. First, Po took it on the chin. The coke was good, so he wasn't tripping on paying 35 a joint. But the last two times the coke wasn't shit. The bitch told Po that Ant was hating on him; however, Po ain't pay that bitch no mind, until he started seeing that shit and had to get him.

"What you about to do?" D.J. asked Ant, seeing him putting eight bricks in a duffle bag.

"I'm bouta drop this shit off to Po's wild ass real quick," Ant said, zipping up the bag and picking it up.

"Hit me soon as you finish, we re-up tomorrow. I'm bouta put my half together now." D.J. told Ant as they walked out the trap. Ant dapped D.J. up and hopped in his Charger, pulling off, calling Po. Po and Savage were posted in Stanton's liquor store. Savage was talking to this pretty, thick bitch named E-Ball, drinking Rosé out the bottle, leaning on the counter, and twisting up a phat ass sheet of gas when Po's phone rung. Po served a junkie, put the money in his pocket, and grabbed his phone, answering it. "I'm pulling up in 15 minutes," Ant told Po and hung up.

"Stop faking," E-ball told Savage, putting her number in his phone. Savage palmed her ass, watching her walk out the store.

"He bout to pull up." Po told Savage as they jogged out the store. Ant pulled up in front of building 1501, texted Po that he was out front, and finished texting the bitch he was trying to fuck later. Savage saw when Ant pulled up, he took off all his jewelry, threw on his mask, with his Glock 22 out as he hopped out the car. He ran up to Ant's car, and caught him with his head down, still texting. "Don't move," Savage demanded, snatching Ant's door open, pulling the trigger, and hitting Ant in his chest. He reached over, grabbed the duffle bag off the passenger seat, and took off up the block.

"Fuck that nigga!" Po said as Savage ran through the back-door, bag in his hand.

A junkie was in the window all day. She owed Po and knew he wasn't giving her shit, so she been mad and geeking all day. She saw when Savage first walked to his car, so when he hopped out, she knew who he was even though he had on his mask. When he shot Ant, she was the one that called the police, putting two and two together, thinking, *I know Po tight ass set that play up!*

SKY

12:10 A.M.

Raven and Megan were getting dressed for the club. Sky put his guns he bought with him all over the house for easy access just in case shit got crazy around there. He brought 75 bands over with him, 10 of which he put in his Balmain, telling Raven to put the rest in the room. Sky ain't put on no shirt. It was too hot. He let his chain be his shirt, rocking all his jewelry with knots poking out his pocket, Glock showing, doing him.

"You ready, baby?" Raven asked as her and Megan walked out the room in some lil ass boy shorts, showing their sexy, thick thighs and phat pussy prints. They both had their book bags on. Sky was dropping them off at the club.

"Yeah, come on," he told them as they walked out the apartment. When they got close to the bottom of the steps, they saw Squirrel and Frank Jones standing at the building door. Drake was nodding on the steps with a cup of lean in his hand.

"Ugggh," Megan said, rolling her eyes as they walked pass Drake. Drake looked up, seeing Megan and Raven with some nigga he didn't know. Raven didn't like none of the niggas around their way and was mad at herself for letting any of them fuck her. She saw everybody watching so she stood on her tippy toes and kissed Sky on his lips. Megan did the same and walked out the building without speaking.

Drake was looking at all that jewelry on Sky. *I got to get him.*

Sky knew that look and pulled out a knot at the same time Tia and Tamia were walking down the steps. "Let me get an ounce and what's up?" Sky greeted Squirrel and Jones as he flipped through his money, knowing Drake was watching. He handed Jones 250 dollars.

Tia and Tamia were observing Sky's tattoos, his knot, his swag all together. They were on his dick after watching him stuff knots back in his Balmain. Jones jogged down to the basement, coming back with an ounce of gas.

"Good looking," Sky said, smelling it. He dapped them up and rambled out the building.

"I got to get him," Drake said to himself, nodding as he took another sip of lean. The perks were kicking in.

"I don't like none of them, baby. I swear I don't," Raven told Sky as they hopped in the truck.

"Shit cool, just lay back… you aiight, Megan?" Sky asked, handling her weed.

"I'm cool," Megan responded.

"Twist up then," Sky told her, smiling as he pulled off, cutting up the music, already baking a cake for all them niggas.

SAVAGE

Savage sat in the trap with Po until 4 in the morning, waiting for the police to leave. Bubbles stayed on the phone with Savage until she fell asleep, telling him about her day and goals. Po was in the kitchen over the pots, whipping all night. Savage went to sleep and woke back up, and Po was still in the kitchen cooking up, throwing blocks up on the scale.

"That shit stink," Savage told him, grabbing his money, looking out the window.

"Yeah, but when I hop in that 2021 Audi A8 all white, that fresh car smell gon' smell good," Po laughed, nodding at Savage. He gave Savage his Taurus 9 and dapped him up and locked the trap up after Savage left out. He walked right back to the kitchen only thing on his mind was running it up.

Savage stopped at McDonald's, purchasing two bacon, egg, and cheese sandwiches and a small orange juice. Savage was eating in his car. *I ain't trying to drive all the way out Woodbridge. Fuck that*, he said to himself, grabbing his phone and calling Sky as he pulled off. Sky was asleep on the couch ass naked. Raven was sleeping on him, legs spread over his waist, his dick still in her. Megan heard Sky's phone ringing as she sat on her Lay•Z•Boy chair smoking, scrolling through her IG page.

"Sky," she called, getting up, grabbing his phone, and shaking him awake.

"Yeah, Megan?" he slurred, looking at her through slit eyes.

"Your phone, boo," she told him, handing Sky his phone. Megan smiled and smacked Raven's ass.

"Stopppp," Raven cried, wrapping her arms around Sky tighter and falling back to sleep.

"Yeah," Sky greeted, answering his phone. "Twist me some gas, Megan," Sky told her.

"Fuck you at?" Savage asked.

"What's up, Slim? I'm up 22nd, apartment 4 building 501. I'm up Raven's joint… we got to talk anyway," Sky told him and hung up. "Get up Raven, huh," Sky told Raven, smacking her ass. Raven sucked her teeth while getting up and grabbing the weed from Sky as he got up and stretched.

"You ain't see none of them niggas this morning?" Sky asked.

"Naw, it's been empty," she said to him.

"Aiight, my man about to pull up so open the door for him," Sky said, grabbing the J from Raven. "I'm bout to take a shower."

"I'm going too," Raven said, following Sky to the bathroom.

"Raven, Sky got your lil ass wide open," Megan hollered before looking back at her I.G. *Hell, I'm falling for this nigga, too.*

Savage pulled up 22nd, parking beside Sky's Range; he put the Taurus in his pocket and grabbed the bag of money. *If a nigga broke in my shit. I can't let 'em get a free 50.*

"Fuck that," he said to himself, hopping out the Ferrari with his hand on his Taurus, walking to building 501. He saw two niggas looking his way as he walked in the building. He trekked up to the apartment and the door opened before he could knock.

"You must be Savage. You cute, come in." Megan told Savage, biting her bottom lip, looking him up and down while standing in the door way in a t-shirt and thong. You could see her phat pussy lips.

"What's up?" Savage greeted, moving into the apartment, smelling bacon and eggs in the air.

"Fuck is up?" Savage greeted, seeing Sky sitting at the living room table with a plate full of food in front him, J burning in the ashtray, and drinking Rosé to wash the food down, with his Glock 17 sitting by the bottle. Sky had on a pair of shorts, all his jewelry on, Dior briefs showing. No shirt on with some Dior slippers on his feet with no socks on. Sky looked at Savage smiling. Raven walked out the kitchen with another plate in her hand. She was in a tank top and boy shorts.

"Hey, Savage," she greeted and sat beside Sky.

"Come sit with me." Megan grabbed Savage's hand, walking him to the lazy chair. She let him sit first, took the Taurus out his pocket and laid it on the floor, and sat her soft ass on his lap.

"This how you living?" Savage asked, dropping the bag, grabbing Megan's thighs, and watching Raven feeding Sky.

"Yeah," Sky told 'em laughing.

BIG MIKE

Big Mike was sitting in his office, thinking between Savage and Sky, they had spent close to 200 bands on cars. He knew Freaky ain't give them no big cuts from the hits. That wasn't

Freaky's style. Freaky was a tight, sneaky, cruddy muthafucka and Big Mike knew this. *I fuck with Savage, and I pray he ain't put his feet in some shit he can't get out of,* Big Mike said to himself, letting his mind wonder.

TYSON

Tyson was still holding shit down. He had just dropped off three bricks to Pat, who had been holding down Montana since Gucci left. Everything was going good for Tyson except his man ain't wake up. Tyson went to the hospital every day. Tone was still in the fight between life and death. Tyson had him in his prayers and made sure Tone's cut got put up every day. Loyalty was big to Tyson and when a person a real nigga, you make sure you stay loyal to him because real niggas were hard to come by. Plus, Tyson lived by and was going to die by that code.

SKY AND SAVAGE

Raven and Megan got dressed. Raven put on an all-white Saint Laurent two piece, and Megan had on a sexy spaghetti strap all-gray Prada dress that stopped at her thighs; both of them had heels on as they walked in the living room posing for Savage and Sky. They knew they looked good.

"Here, baby," Sky said, handing both of them five bands a piece.

"Thank you," Raven said, kissing his lips as he palmed her ass.

"I got my eyes open. I got you, baby," Megan said, kissing Savage on the lips.

"Bye, Savage," they both said, Megan winked and licked her tongue at him as they left out the apartment.

"It's two niggas around here named Jones and Squirrel. Megan say they up. Her and Raven used to fuck them niggas and shit. Squirrel still got a thing for Megan on the low even doe he got a bitch," Sky told Savage grinning.

"The niggas Jones' and Squirrel's bitches on my dick… I'ma fuck 'em when I catch 'em dolo. We gon' snatch both them niggas." Sky laughed and laid back on the couch.

"The nigga be off perks and lean, nodding. I'ma catch 'em with his head in his lap and fuck him around. Megan, say he got a couple niggas named Rob and Sam. I ain't see 'em yet, but I'ma flush they ass too," Sky said in a calm voice.

"What's up with Raven and Megan? Which one you on?" Savage asked, looking at Sky, thinking, *this nigga purpin'.*

"Both of them my bitches, but Raven, that's *my baby.* That's me… I'm falling for her lil ass," Sky told him laughing.

"Megan's my baby too but I ain't tripping off her for real… I'm a still fuck and shit but that's more like my partner. She a lil bit seasoned on this street shit than my baby Raven, but I fuck with both of them," Sky said seriously.

"I'm tryna fuck Megan, what's up?" Savage said.

"Go head, Slim… you can't fuck Raven doe," Sky told him.

"I'm hip. I see how y'all hugged up and kissing and shit. She feeding you, going everywhere you go. I see on the low, Slim." Savage told him laughing.

"Yeah, that's my bitch," Sky told him.

Savage's phone rung. He grabbed it, reading a text from Bubbles, telling him he needed to be home in the next 2 hours. Savage laughed, stood, grabbed his bag, and put the Taurus back in his pocket.

"Hit me when you ready. I got to get home or I'ma be on punishment," Savage told Sky, dapping him up.

"Aiight, Moe. Love you, Slim," Sky told him as Savage left out the apartment. "Yeah, I'ma rob all these niggas around here. It's only right," Sky said to himself, laying back on the couch plotting.

CHAPTER EIGHTEEN

DETECTIVE ROB AND GRAM

"Listen, I've got information on Sky, Savage, and Freaky," Detective Rob told his team, pointing to three pictures hanging on the board in the conference room.

"I have an address for Freaky, but my informant doesn't think he is staying at the apartment anymore. I've called the F.B.I. for a lil help. We're hitting the whole complex at 4:00a.m., each unit is going to be assigned to a building… we hit hard and fast. I have a strong feeling Freaky's living in one of them apartments so be ready. Meeting's over." Detective Rob told his team and looked towards Gram. "Let's get him first then take down the rest of these muthafucka!!!"

FREAKY

"Shit, fuck my ass you big dick, black motherfucker." Alexis Sky screamed. Freaky was laid back on the couch, beating his dick while watching the porno. He was horny as shit, wanting to try out all the positions on somebody.

DRAKE

Drake, Sam, and Rob were sitting in the trap across the street from Raven's building pouring lean, all of them off perks high as shit. Drake was standing by the window watching Sky walk out the building. He put Sam and Rob on point about who he was. They were ready to brace Sky right then. They saw him with all that jewelry on and knew he was a lick.

Drake calmed them down, telling them to chill, "We gon' get him for everything. We got to kill him, now… he ain't just one of them niggas you rob and ain't gon' do shit."

"We going to get him and I'ma smack the shit out of Raven, too. Bitch actin' like she ain't a thot. I just fucked for $200 a month ago," Sam vented, taking a sip of lean. "I'ma see what's up with her and if she purpin', I'ma smack the shit out of her and I want Slim to say something," Sam said, dapping Rob up.

Drake was sipping his cup plotting on getting Sky.

SKY

In her voice, baby, you… why you got to thug on me? Why you can't just love on me? Moneybagg blasted out the Range Sport as Sky pulled up beside Beauty's Lexus at Applebee's parking lot. Beauty was shaking her head. *Look at my lil fuckin' brother.* Sky turned the song all the way up and hopped out singing. "Fuck her thoughts, you ain't been crossed, took no loss, you ain't no boss, fuck you thought, murder talk." Sky sung with Bagg nodding his head, looking sweet in a hitting ass sky blue Balenciaga fitted sweatsuit. He had all his jewelry on and a compact 40 in his sweatpants pocket. He smiled at his sister. Cutting off the truck, he grabbed a bookbag off the seat, closed the door, and walked to Beauty's Lex truck. A couple females were watching him, wondering who he was and if the girl in the Lex was his girl.

"Because if not, I'm all over that," Beauty told Sky smiling as he handed her the bag of money.

"That's 50… you know my shit be purpin' on these wild niggas. What's up with you?" Sky asked, laying his seat back, watching his sister sliding the bag under the seat.

"Nothing laid back… you know me but what's up with your lil friend Savage?" she asked, looking over at him.

"Come on sis, we don't be saving nothing," he told her laughing, his eyes focused on two niggas hopping out the Audi, watching them walking in Applebee's. "He put that dick on you, got yo shit geekin'."

"Boy, stop fucking playing with me… you know how sis do. I was just asking." Beauty lied, rolling her eyes. She was really on Savage's dick and wanted to see him bad.

"Anyway," Beauty said, changing the subject, "where your girlfriend at?"

"Which one? I got two. We live together." Sky said, looking in Beauty's face.

"Never mind. What are you going do about this police stuff, Sky? I got your back but goddamn, you just beat a murder, and now you're in fucking trouble again… you a trip, lil boy." Beauty pushed Sky's head, shaking hers. *I love my brother but he just fucking bad.*

"They got to catch me, sis. I'm doing me, fuck all that… let's go eat. I'm hungry as shit." Sky told her not really trying to hear that preaching shit.

"I'm going to still talk about it. Nobody care about your lil attitude." Beauty said behind his back, following him in Applebee's.

RAVEN AND MEGAN

Raven and Megan pulled in their parking lot, grabbed their bags, and hopped out the car. It was lit in the Courts, everybody was outside cooling, gas smoke was in the air as kids ran around playing. Sam, Rob, Squirrel, and Jones were sitting in front of the building. As they walked, Raven sucked her teeth as they got close.

"There go Raven lil sexy ass, her and Megan." Rob watched them walking up the sidewalk; looking at their thighs, his dick was getting hard thinking, *these bitches like that*.

Squirrel looked around for his girl Tia and turned to Jones. "Slim, I got to fuck Megan again… I got to get some more of that pussy."

Jones laughed, looking at Raven and Megan thinking, *I'm trying fuck the bitches too*.

"Damn, Raven," Sam said, grabbing Raven's arm as she walked by, pulling her to him, and palming her ass. "What's up Raven? I'm trying see what that pussy do again."

"Boy, get the fuck on," Raven yelled, everybody was watching as she snatched her arm away. "I got a dude. Plus, your lil dick ass broke," she said looking him up and down. *I don't know why I ever let him fuck me*. Everybody was watching and laughing. Sam was embarrassed, getting mad as shit.

"Bitch, fuck you! Everybody fucked your anything ass. Now you fuck with that wild ass nigga Sky, you think you like that, bitch you anything," Sam snapped and smacked the shit out of Raven.

"Ahhh," Raven screamed, holding her face.

"You a bitch, hitting a girl, bitch ass nigga. I got something for you, bitch ass nigga… watch." Megan told Sam, walking in the building behind Raven.

"Bitch, fuck y'all thot ass," Sam yelled, grabbing the J

from Rob. Rob was laughing like shit. Jones and Squirrel just shook their heads thinking this nigga lunchin'.

"Bitch ass niggas!" Raven cried, looking at her face and seeing her lip was split open. "I got his ass," she told Megan again, grabbing her phone and calling Sky.

"THEM GIRLS LOOKING at you on the lows. They must think I'm your girl." Beauty told Sky as he ate a wing, washing it down with his drink.

"Where they at?" Sky asked, licking barbecue sauce off his fingers.

"Them," Beauty pointed the girls way. Sky looked and blew both of them a kiss, they blushed and blew kisses back geeking, when his phone started ringing.

"Boy, you too much," Beauty said, taking a sip of her drink; she was having fun watching Sky answering his phone.

"Boo," Raven greeted soon as Sky answered, he heard her crying and asked what's up, hanging onto his pocket not even knowing it.

"Sam smacked me." Raven told him and busted out crying. "He split my fucking lip," she yelled, looking at her lip in the mirror.

"Where he at?" Sky asked in murder mode, standing up.

"What's wrong, Sky?" Beauty asked, knowing that look.

"I'm on my way." Sky hung up, dropping the 50's on the table. "I'm gone sis,' he told Beauty, kissed her cheek, and jogged out the restaurant, dialing Savage's number.

The two girls walked up to Beauty's table and handed her their numbers, asking could she give it to the guy that had just left. Beauty smiled, grabbed the numbers, and said a quick prayer knowing Sky was on his shit.

SAVAGE

"You like this, baby?" Bubbles asked, pointing to a king size bed. Savage and Bubbles had been out shopping all day.

"It's cool, boo… you know I ain't really good at this shit. I like what you like." Savage said, pulling Bubbles to him by her ass, kissing her lips.

"You no fun," she said, kissing him back. "I like this. I want it. Let me go get the store clerk," she told Savage and walked off, throwing her ass knowing Savage was watching.

"Damn," Savage said to himself when his phone rung. He watched Bubbles walk to the store clerk at the counter as he answered. "What's up Slim?"

"Go get the Drako. Niggas purpin'… flush season right now," Sky said, doing the dash back to the city.

"Bet," Savage told him, hanging up, looking at Bubbles, knowing she was about to be beefing.

"What?" she asked, knowing that look.

"Shit bad with Sky… we got to come back later, boo, flat out." He grabbed her hand, walking out the store. The clerk just watched, thinking, *I thought we had a deal closed.*

Making it back to Bubbles whip, they hopped in and Bubbles crunk it up.

"You get on my fucking nerves, Savage; you and Sky owe me, and I want mine," Bubbles screeched, pulling off. All on Savage's mind was getting the chopstick out. *Niggas got my man fucked up.*

SKY

Sky called Raven before he pulled up and asked what the nigga had on. Raven told' em while looking out the window, seeing he was still outside. Sky hung up, parked, and hopped out, took out his 40, and walked in the Courts. "I wish a nigga would try me. I don't give a fuck who it is," Sam told Rob. Jones and Squirrel were sitting on the steps. Tia and Tamia were sitting on their laps. "Aye, Squirrel!" somebody called, seeing Sky walking up with the 40 in his hand.

"Aye Sam," Squirrel called but it was too late. Sky grabbed him by his shirt and smacked him in his face with the 40. Sam fell on the gate. Sky was still smacking him. Blood was flying on his clothes. Rob was stuck, snapped out of it, and tried to reach. Sky turned, putting the 40 in his face as Sam fell on the ground, face leaking.

"I wish you would. I'll flush yo bitch ass…. put your

hands up." Sky kicked him in his face and took the dog off his hip. The whole neighborhood was watching.

"Hold up," Squirrel yelled, getting up. "Ease up, Slim. Shit too hot… you do anything you go to jail. Point made, Slim," Squirrel pleaded, seeing that look in his eyes.

"Don't *nobody* touch my bitches. I don't give a fuck what they do, bitch ass nigga," Sky yelled and stepped up the porch, walking in the building.

Rob helped Sam to his feet, saw his jaw was hanging as blood was pouring down his face. Sam was dizzy as Rob helped him walk off. "We goin' to war bout that shit. I promise." Rob said to himself, helping his man walk up the back. Tia and Tamia were in shock; they never saw nobody step to Sam like that. They both were on Sky's dick.

"It's gon' be a lot of gun fire bout that shit. It's gon' be hot as shit around here, watch. Fuckin' with Drake. I know he told Sam to do that bum ass shit to Raven." Squirrel vented to Jones, thinking, *I ain't getting with that!*

Raven and Megan were in the window watching Sky pistol whipping the shit out Sam. "That's what his bitch ass get." Raven saw Sky walking in the building and walked to the door to meet him.

Megan was watching Rob help Sam up the block, thinking, *this nigga Sky don't play.* She turned to the sound of the door closing, seeing Sky carrying Raven in the living room.

Megan shook her head, saying, "Raven lil ass in love." She had never seen her on a nigga like she was on Sky.

Sky sat on the couch with Raven still on his lap. She took off his bloody shirt, sat the guns on the table, glaring in Sky's face with love in her eyes.

"You aiight?" Sky asked, kissing Raven's split lip.

"Yes. Thank you, Daddy," Raven told him, rubbing his face.

"Shit ain't nothing. What's up, Megan?" he greeted smiling.

"You," Megan said grinning.

"Twist up, fireworks are about to go off in minute. Let's enjoy the show." He told her as Raven laid her head on his shoulders. She was in love with Sky.

Soon as Savage got close to 22nd, he called Sky and asked, "Who is the nigga?"

"One bloody with red on… the other one a black ass nigga with dreads. Matter fact, Raven bout to send you pictures of both of them," Sky told him and hung up.

DRAKE

Rob hit Drake and let him know what the fuck just happened. Drake was out VA with his cousin Keem seeing their aunt. "We killin' that nigga soon as I get back. I'm bout to take Sam to the hospital. His shit broke. I'ma hit you soon as I pull up," Rob said and hung up.

Keem heard the whole conversation. "What's up? You want me and Lil E to pull up and flush somethin'?"

"Naw, I got it. Shit light work." Drake told him only if he knew Keem was beefing with the same nigga.

Savage parked down the block, put the drako under his trench coat, and his hat down low over his eyes. He looked at the pictures one more time and hopped out the car, walking up 22nd on a mission. Rob and Sam left the building. Sam was hurting, mad as shit. The only thing on his mind was killing Sky as they walked to the parking lot.

SAVAGE

Savage was walking up the courts, when he walked pass Rob and Sam. Rob looked at Savage wondering why the fuck, he had on a trench coat when it was 80 degrees outside.

"Dumb ass nigga." Rob said, walking down the steps.

Savage's heartbeat started racing as he put his hand around the trigger, turned around, and started following Rob and Sam down the steps. Rob turned around seeing the dude in the trench walking their way.

"What the fuck?" was all Rob got to say before Savage pulled the trigger and shot through the coat.

Blocka! Blocka! Blocka! Blocka! Blocka!

Shots rang out as the first bullets chopped Rob down. Sam tried to run, but bullets were hitting him all in his back and head.

People were running as shots sounded like an army was in

the area. Savage put a couple more in the back of Sam's head and took off running up the block.

SKY

Sky was smoking a phat ass sheet of gas. He smiled when the shots went off. Raven and Megan looked at Sky and ran out the house to see what the fuck happened. They got to the parking lot to find a crowd around. When Raven and Megan got to the front of the crowd they almost threw up after looking at all the blood and noticing Rob's and Sam's dead bodies stretched out. The back of Sam's skull was open. You could see his brains from the back.

Sky stepped out of the building and walked on the front porch blowing gas. He wanted people to see his face, so they didn't call the police saying he did it. He got a text from Savage, he read it, smiling.

Savage: *Flush Season Savage Life*.

Sky smiled, watching Raven walking his way. He watched Squirrel stop Megan, as Raven grabbed his hand, walking him back in the building.

CHAPTER NINETEEN

DRAKE

*D*rake pulled up 22nd and saw the parking lot was taped off with detectives and plain clothes officers everywhere. Drake had the dog on him, so he parked down the block wondering what the fuck was going on. Drake tried Sam's and Rob's numbers. Both their phones were going to voicemail. Drake tried Squirrel's number. Squirrel was out Maryland at Cheeta's with Megan eating. He saw Drake calling, but ain't answer. He ain't want to be the one to break the news to him. Plus, on the low, he was happy them niggas got killed. They were in the way making the block hot. He wanted Drake dead, too. He and Jones even talked about it but were reluctant to buss a move due to them being Keem and Tyson folks. All the same, they was hoping Sky crushed his ass.

Drake tried Jones' number. Shit had been hot up 22nd since Sam and Rob got flushed. So, after receiving a call from Drake, Jones slid uptown to fuck with Ra'key up CHV.

"Hold up," he told Ra'key, setting the cards down as he answered the phone. "Drake, shit got bad Moe. Sam and Rob got flushed today."

"Killed?" Drake said, his heart dropping in his chest while sitting in his car, hurting hearing that.

"Yeah, Slim. I been uptown all day… niggas don't know who the fuck did that shit. They had a lil situation with the dude Sky, but Sky went to Raven's joint and niggas say a dude in a trench coat and hat low flushed them."

"Fucckkk!" Drake yelled, hanging up, dropping his head, and crying his eyes out.

"Fuck them niggas… bet 100 on the hand," Jones said, picking up his cards as Ra'key put down $100.

MEGAN

Megan stayed out with Squirrel until 3 in the morning, teasing Squirrel all night but didn't give him no pussy. When they pulled up on 22nd, Megan sucked his dick in the parking lot to keep him geeking; she kissed his dick one more time and hopped out his car, throwing her ass, knowing he was watching as that muthafucka was clapping. She ain't have on no draws. You could see her ass cheeks through the dress.

"She know what the fuck she doing," Squirrel said to his self as he put his dick back in his pants. Squirrel looked around still seeing blood stains on the ground.

"Them niggas bullshittin'," he said and pulled off thinking, *better them than me.*

Megan walked to the building and shook her head, seeing Drake in a nod sitting on the steps, cup of lean sitting next to him.

"Dirty ass nigga," Megan said to herself, moving around him up the steps. Megan opened the door, hearing moaning. She smiled, pussy getting wet as she shut and locked the door. She walked to the living room, noticing two empty bottles of Rosé sitting on the table; she grabbed the half-finished J out the ashtray, fired it up, dropped her purse, sauntering to the sound of the moaning. She stepped in the room and leaned on the door watching Sky pushing Raven's knees by her ears, grinding in her pussy.

"Skyyy, it's in this pussy, Daddy," Raven moaned loud.

"Shhhhh," Sky whispered in her ear, sucking her neck, putting his dick in her stomach.

"Skyyy… Ohhh… Skyyy," Raven screamed, cumming all over his dick. She pulled Sky in her deeper as he came deep in her, still grinding in that good pussy.

"Can I have some?" Megan asked, horny as shit, watching Sky's dick as he pulled out of Raven's creamy pussy.

"What's up Megan? How shit go and let me hit that?" Sky told Megan, sitting on the side of the bed drained. Raven's pussy was a torch and they been fucking all night. Raven was on cloud nine, she greeted Megan and climbed under the covers, tired as shit from all that dick.

"It went good. He on a bitch line. I sucked his dick to keep him geeking," she told Sky, handing him the J, taking a seat beside him on the bed.

"Drake in the hallway high as shit off the lean, head in his lap like always. Clown ass nigga," she let him know, shaking her head, grabbing Sky's dick, jerking it up and down slowly. She looked in Sky's eyes and asked, "Can you fuck me to sleep, too? I'm jealous." Megan told Sky and looked at Raven. Raven rolled her eyes grinning, too tired to talk.

"Hold up. Go get my gun," he told Megan, hitting the J a couple more times as he stood up, putting his sweats, shirt, and shoes on. Megan jogged out the room and came back with his Glock and he handed her the J back.

"Who else you see?" Sky asked, cocking the Glock.

"Nobody," she told him, watching him walk out the room, already knowing what's up.

"You having all the fun. That dick good, ain't it?" Megan asked, crawling on the bed, looking Raven in her eyes. Raven smiled and nodded.

"You pressed. I'm getting some. Fuck that," Megan told her and kissed Raven's lips, putting her tongue in Raven's mouth. Megan took off her dress and walked in the living room. Sky was going to give her some dick.

Sky walked pass Drake and stepped out the building, scanning around as he strolled to the end of the Courts; he turned round after seeing nobody was around and walked back to the building. Sky took the Glock off his hip, slinked in the building, looking around, and kicked Drake's drink on the floor.

"Fuck," Drake slurred and looked up.

Sky pulled the trigger.

Boom!

Drake's head hit the back of the steps.

Boom!

Sky shot him again. and ran up the steps, running in the house, shutting and locking the door; he took off all his clothes and jogged to the kitchen, stopping when he noticed Megan on the couch looking at him, fingering herself.

"Fuck me pleaseee," Megan moaned, looking in Sky's face. Sky ran and grabbed a trash bag and some bleach, went into the bathroom, and put the clothes in the tub, drowning them with bleach. Next, he wiped down the Glock, wrapped it up in a towel, and put everything in the trash bag. After going to the bedroom and slipping on some more clothes, he ran to the door and stepped in the hallway, not seeing anyone. He broke out the backdoor, running up the block buildings up and throwing the bag in a big green trash can. When he got back nobody had yet to come investigate the shooting. He walked in the house, locked the door, got ass naked, and walked to the living room.

"This what you want?" Sky grabbed Megan by her waist, made her bend over the couch, and jammed his dick in her pussy, hitting the bottoms.

"Skyyy," Megan screamed as Sky crushed her pussy.

"O my Goddd!" an older lady getting off from work screamed, walking in the building, seeing all that blood, and Drake laid out on the steps, eyes still open.

PO

"Let me get 3 for 100," crackhead Pete asked, handing Po the money. Po served him. "Aye, the junkie bitch Jackie saying she saw your friend kill a dude the other day in front the building. She said you might have pulled the play. The shit was on the news. They asking for info and willing to pay three thousand for it, I'm just putting you on point," the junkie told Po. Po gave the junkie three more 50's, thanked him and watched him walk out the building.

Po walked back in the trap, plotting. *She got to die.*

FREAKY

Freaky got dressed at 3:58 a.m., throwing on all black. The only thing on his mind was grabbing a woman tonight. He made his mind up; he was getting a sex slave.

Freaky looked out the window. "O shit!" He yelled, seeing police cars, SWAT, and the F.B.I. cruisers riding in the parking lot. He saw officers hop out, running to different buildings.

Freaky panicked, grabbing his drako and bag of money. He ran out the apartment, breaking out the backdoor of the building and saw a flash.

Pap!

A bullet hit him in his face and his body hit the ground.

Pap! Pap!

"Perverted motherfucker," Pam's father said and ran off.

Pam's father had been watching Freaky's routine. The first time he peeped Freaky was a week ago. Pam's father was out back putting the trash can in the alley and was shocked that Freaky was still staying in the neighborhood with his face all over the news. That morning, he looked at his watch and seeing it was 3:30 a.m. before he stepped back in the house. Every morning since then, around 2 or 3 a.m., he was plotting, discovering that Freaky was leaving out of the house the same time each morning.

Pam's father was lying in Freaky's bushes waiting patiently. He had been hiding since 2 in the morning. When he checked his watch, it was 4:00 a.m. He started thinking he picked the wrong night until he heard footsteps and saw Freaky and crushed him.

"Bitch ass nigga. I hate them perverted motherfuckers," Pam's father said to himself, wiping the 44 down. He breathed a sigh of relief, knowing Freaky wouldn't be fucking his daughter and she was safe. Officers heard the shot and ran with their guns out. Detective Rob led the pack to the sounds of the shots. He saw a man down, bleeding out with a gun and duffle bag lying beside him.

"Suspect down. It's the fucking suspect!" Detective Rob yelled, kicking away the gun, looking down at Freaky's dead face.

The nurse was coming back in the building from taking her smoke break. She talked to a few people making small talk when the emergency lights went off, calling out the room where she was working. The nurse ran to the room freezing in the doorway, covering her mouth in shock, seeing Tone looking at her alert.

"It's a miracle," she said to herself and ran to get the doctor. "Welcome back, Tone!!"

SKY

Sky pulled up 22nd, parking in the parking lot. After he crushed Drake, and with Sam and Rob getting flushed, 22nd was hot as shit; police was up there every day trying to get answers. Sky got Megan and Raven and rented out a house. When they came back around shit was cool. Niggas couldn't say, but they had an idea Sky had something to do with Drake, Rob, and Sam getting crushed. Niggas ain't want no work.

Keem and Lil E came around asking questions, dogged up,

wanting smoke, but ain't nobody know nothing. Sky's name wasn't even mentioned. They was staying out that shit. Plus, most people around the way was happy they were dead; they were some cruddy motherfuckers.

Sky hopped out with his Gucci bubble trench coat open, showing his all-platinum choker with the I.F.L. pendant. Dark blue Zora skinny's with the Gucci belt on; double G showing, double sole butters on his feet, 5th on his hip.

He shut the door and walked in the Courts. Tia was sitting on Squirrel's lap; she saw Sky from afar and told Squirrel that she was bout to use the bathroom. Tia got up and walked in the building.

"What's up?" he greeted, looking at her.

"What's up, Sky. Where's Raven?" she asked, lust in her eyes, looking at Sky. *This nigga always looking sweet.*

"Her and Megan out somewhere. You know I just bought them the Lex so their geekin'. I be back. I'm tryna get an O of gas, Moe." Sky told Jones and stepped in the building. Sky was stepping up the steps and heard his name being called. He turned around and saw Tia waving him over, standing in her doorway in just a tank top, pussy showing.

"Come here," she whispered, looking towards the building door for Squirrel. Sky grinned looking towards the building door before walking to Tia. Soon as he stepped in, he dropped his pants, Glock falling on the ground as he pulled out his dick. Tia pulled him into the living room by his dick, bent over the couch, and looked over her shoulder at Sky. Tia had a nice, small, shaved, pretty pussy.

"Ohhh," she moaned as Sky slid his raw dick in her tight wet pussy.

"This what you want?" Sky asked, spreading her ass, fucking the shit out her pussy.

"Yess, it's what I want," she moaned, biting her lip as he hit her soft spot. Sky grabbed her waist and went to work her ass jiggled every time it hit her pelvis.

"Sky, Ohhh Sky… right there… you hitting my spot," she screamed, cumming all over his dick. Sky pulled out and spread her ass cheeks, nutting all over her asshole, smacking his dick all on her asshole. He pulled his pants up, smacked her soft ass and walked off, picking his Glock up and walking out the apartment heading to his whip thinking, *these bitches on a nigga's dick*.

He took off his coat, grabbed his phone, and texted Raven, telling her to bring him a bottle of Rosé as he walked in the bathroom washing his dick. He walked out the apartment counting out 250 as he stepped out the building, laughing to his self, seeing Tia sitting on Squirrel's lap. Squirrel was kissing her neck. She glanced at Sky on the low, wanting some more of that dick. Sky bought the ounce and walked back in the building.

"Can't wait till Megan say it's a go. These niggas anything," he said to himself in the house, locking the door behind him.

"LOOK AT YOU, slim… you skinny as a motherfucker, ugly ass," Tyson told Tone excited, happy as shit his man was alive and alert.

"Fuck you," Tone said in a hoarse voice. He was on a piss and shit bag, had to have a lung removed plus additional surgery to remove all the bullets that were in his body. Tone was shot 18 times in his head, face, and body. For Tone to be alive, talking, alert, and breathing on his own was nothing short of a miracle.

"Fuck all that, doe. Did the bitch Bubbles set you up?" Tyson asked seriously, looking in Tone's face.

"Naw, she called the police, slim. If it wasn't for that, I'll be dead," Tone told Tyson. "It was the nigga Savage and some other nigga in the picture you sent me that day."

"What?" Tyson was shocked, wondering how the fuck them bitch ass niggas got up on him like that.

"That's some inside shit, slim. I know it was," Tyson stressed.

"Look, get Big Mike the pictures of both them niggas and drop off 200 bands. Find out them niggas family members. I want their whole bloodline dead. Other than you and Big Mike, no one is to know I'm alive. Clean up. I'm done playing these stupid ass games," Tone said, looking in Tyson's eyes.

"I'm on it." Tyson pulled out his phone, calling Keem and Lil E.

"Clean up. Smoke the bitch," He told Keem and hung up. Shit was about to become real.

DETECTIVE ROB AND GRAM

Detective Rob and Gram pulled up Iverson Mall parking lot, parking beside an all-black Tahoe truck. Nook hopped out, looking both ways seeing who was watching, and hopped in the back of Rob's unmarked police car.

"Nook, how's it been? You're lookin' better, face healing up nice," Detective Gram told Nook, making small talk.

"I'm cool, glad that piece of shit Freaky got killed. I wish I could've spit in his face," Nook said with a disgusted look on his face.

"We're about to put Savage's and Sky's faces on the news. Apply some pressure. You're willing to testify," Detective Rob asked, turning in his seat and looking in Nook's face.

"Yeah, fuck them niggas," Nook told him, looking back in Detective Rob's eyes.

BUBBLES

"Open your mouth," Bubbles told Savage, feeding him some crab meat dipped in butter.

Bubbles and Savage were sitting on the balcony. She bought a bunch of crabs and shrimp and had gas sitting in a glass bowl. Savage was drinking Rosé, Bubbles was drinking

Patrón, and she was in a gray one piece fitted tight on her body, making her camel toe press against the fabric. Her hair was hanging down her back, and she wore no socks or shoes on her pretty feet. Bubbles was looking good.

Savage ate the crab meat and laid back in the lawn chair. He smacked Bubbles' ass watching it jiggle as he grabbed the J out the ashtray. Bubbles wiped off her hands and sat on Savage's lap.

"Savage, I got something to tell you," she said, grabbing the J out of Savage's hand, putting it in the ashtray. Savage blew smoke in the air and looked at Bubbles. *She think she runnin' shit.*

"I'm pregnant," she told Savage, examining his face to see his expression. She already had in her mind if Savage said anything stupid, she was going to fuck him up. She already positioned herself and was ready.

Savage looked at her, making her sweat. He already knew. He saw the test in the trash last night. Plus, she'd been too happy all day. He was just waiting on her to say something.

"So, you not gon' say shit? You know what? Fuck you, Savage," Bubbles' eyes was watery as she tried to get up and walk off.

"Come here," Savage laughed, hugging, and kissing her face.

"I'm happy, baby… we having a lil boy, young Savage" he told her, wiping the tears from her face and kissing her lips.

Bubbles smiled, kissing him back.

"We having a girl," she told him, looking in his eyes. "I love you, Trey. I love you so fucking much," she admitted, standing up, grabbing Savage's hand, and pulling him to his feet. Savage grabbed the J as Bubbles pulled him in the house. She was going to give him some pussy.

CHAPTER TWENTY

BEAUTY

*B*eauty been going on a couple dates, but she really missed Dave and was mad at herself; she let lust and good dick cloud her judgment. She was hurt that she hurt Dave. She pulled up at home at 12:00p.m. with Dave on her mind. She didn't know that Sky tried to kill Dave or that Dave put a hit on all of them. She texted Dave *"sorry"* as she hopped out the car, grabbing her purse. She was looking at her phone while walking to the building, hoping Dave would text back.

She strode into her building and walked pass a light skin guy sitting on the hallway steps messing with his phone. They made eye contact, Keem nodded, then put his head back in his phone as Beauty walked pass. Putting the phone back in his pocket and grabbing his Glock, Keem stood up and trailed behind Beauty. Beauty had her head down, smiling while reading the text when she felt the Glock to her head. Wasting no time, Keem pulled the trigger.

POW!

Blood flew all over the door as Keem broke out the building. Beauty's body fell on the top of her phone.

Dave has just texted back that he missed her, too.

"YOU ALWAYS DRINKING ROSÉ, TASTE THIS…" Raven told Sky, sitting on his lap in her living room, handing him a drink.

"Fuck is this?" Sky asked, taking the drink. "This shit look too cute." Sky told her, looking at it.

"Boy, just drink it," Raven said, smiling, shaking her head. Sky took a sip, then drunk it all, handing Raven back the glass.

"Sky, taste, not drink it all." Raven rolled her eyes and got up to fix another one.

"Fix me one of them mother…" Sky was about to finish when the news caught his eyes.

"This is D.C. News. A young woman, age 27, named Beauty Keys was gunned down tonight in Columbia, MD, at the Quiet Hours Apartment complex. She was shot in the back of the head. Police found her dead on the scene."

Sky was in shock, confused, just staring at the T.V. as tears were pouring down his face. He jumped up, kicked the table over, and punched the wall. Raven was standing in the kitchen doorway watching Sky, confused. Sky slid down the wall, tears flowing freely down his face. Raven walked up to him, grabbed his phone, and dialed a number. Raven was hurting, crying after seeing him crying.

"Hello," Savage slurred, laying in the bed. Bubbles was sleeping, her head resting on Savage's chest.

"Slim, niggas crushed Beauty. slim, I'm hurting bout that shit… shit crazy. I'm killing any nigga that looked, said, or thought some hating shit, slim," Sky vowed as Raven wiped his face.

"Damn," Savage mumbled, getting out the bed. He was fucked up after hearing that shit.

"What's wrong?" Bubbles asked, seeing the look on Savage's face.

"Sky's sister got killed," he told her.

"Where you at? I'm bouta pull up. I'm getting dressed now," Savage told him, grabbing his P89 and Bubbles' car keys.

"Up Raven's joint," Sky said and hung up. Raven got down and climbed in Sky's lap, kissing his lips as she wrapped her arms around him crying. Tears slid down Sky's face as he hugged her back, and a new type of killer came to life.

BIG MIKE

Big Mike was sitting in his office at his desk, glancing down at a picture of Savage and Sky. Tyson had dropped it off earlier that day, telling him that's who shot up Tone. All Big Mike could do was shake his head.

I had a feeling. "Damn, I fuck with Savage's lil ass. You stepped in the big leagues and did some rookie shit, not making sure your target was dead. Now my back is against the wall and shit bout to get ugly," Big Mike said to himself, reflecting at the pictures.

DAVE

When Dave left the city, he went out to VA with his cousin, Fat Tone, out of Norfolk, VA with the dope Tyson gave him and was doing numbers. Dave was fucking all the bitches in the city but still thought about Beauty every now and then. So, when she texted, she was sorry, all his feelings started coming back, and he started to regret the decision he made. He texted her back but didn't get a response. He knew Sky was trying to kill him, but he said fuck it, he was going to see his bitch. He hopped in the car and drove all the way to the city. When Dave pulled into Beauty's parking lot, he saw police everywhere. Her building was tapped off, and people was standing outside, watching the scene as he parked. Dave hopped out and walked to the crowd.

"What happened?" he asked two females that were standing at the tape watching.

"Some bitch ass, soft ass nigga killed a girl. I knew the girl, too. Her lil brother was cute as shit," the other girl said giggling.

"What was the girl's name?" Dave asked, already having an idea.

"I think they call her Sexy or Beauty. Yeah, it was Beauty. She drove the white Lex," one girl told Dave.

Dave walked off, tears rolling down his face as he hopped in his car, emotions getting the best of him asl. He called Tyson.

Tyson, Keem, and Lil E were sitting in his office in Exits watching the news when Tyson's phone rang. Tyson grabbed the phone off the table and answered.

"You killed her, slim. Why you kill her?" Dave asked crying.

"Hold, hold... I ain't do shit!" Tyson said, steaming that Dave was talking like that over his main line.

"Meet me at your old house, we got to talk asap," Tyson told him, eyeballing Keem and Lil E.

"Aiight." Dave wiped his face and pulled off with a heavy heart.

"I can't trust this nigga. Flush him when you see me talking to him," Tyson told Keem and Lil E as he walked to his car mad as shit at these weak ass niggas.

SKY AND SAVAGE

"I know Dave's bitch ass had something to do with that shit. They killed *my heart*, slim. They killed sis," Sky vented, hitting the J, tears rolling down his face.

Him and Savage were sitting in Raven's parking lot in Bubbles' 650 Maybach Coupe blowing gas. Tears were coming down Savage's face, too, feeling Sky's pain.

"Everybody dead, Moe. Beauty got to go out in style, slim. All-white shit, horses, all that shit. Sis got to go like the queen she was," Sky told Savage.

Seriously, both of them were high as shit. He was on his 10th J and didn't plan on stopping, either.

"We going to make sure that shit happens. I'ma get Bubbles to set that shit up asap. I got you," Savage told him, laying his seat back with his Glock on his lap, cooling with his man until Sky was ready to leave.

DAVE PULLED UP OUT LANDOVER, MD to his old apartment waiting on Tyson. He had some words for him. Dave was mad at Tyson and himself.

"I shoulda never did this shit. Fucckkk!" Dave yelled, banging his fist on the steering wheel. Dave's mind wasn't on nothing, but Beauty getting killed so he never saw two dudes running up to his car until shots rang out.

Blocka! Blocka! Blocka! Blocka!

Glass broke as Dave got hit all in his head. They both turned and ran to their car as Dave died, body bleeding out, head laying on the steering wheel.

Tyson was mad the nigga Dave said that hot ass shit on his phone. He ain't even want to talk to the nigga.

He waited until Dave pulled in the parking lot, called Keem and Lil E, and told them what car Dave was in. He left the scene but heard shots.

"Fuck that nigga," he said, cutting up the music, and headed back to the city. He had shit to do.

Squirrel finally took Megan to where he laid his head at. Megan slipped a couple pills in the drink and sucked and fucked him until he was sleep. Making sure he was knocked out, Megan searched his house, finding his stash. She smiled. She couldn't wait to let her baby Sky know they caught them ducks lackin'.

DETECTIVE ROB AND GRAM

The detectives had Lil D and Nook's statements and with Beauty getting killed, they knew the streets were about to get crazy. They got in touch with all the local news stations and gave them Sky's and Savage's picture, letting them know they were armed, dangerous, and wanted for more than six murders and attempted murders. It was a fifty thousand dollar reward for any information on their arrest.

CHAPTER TWENTY-ONE

*B*ubbles woke up and made all the arrangements for Beauty's funeral. She had a big day today. Waking Savage, she took a shower.

She was excited everything was going good for her. It was unfortunate that her man's right hand had lost his sister, but she didn't know her so she was unfazed, singing as she stood in front of her full length mirror getting dressed.

Bubbles put on some Paul Smith gray slacks that fit her ass and thighs tight. She looked good in them.

She threw on a pair of Christian Louboutin heels, and an all-white Berluti blouse, under which she wore no bra. She tucked her blouse in her slacks, and unbuttoned the top two buttons, showing her cleavage.

Bubbles' dreads were done in a crown. She put a women's Rolex on her wrist, and a nice chain with a heart pendant that

Savage got for her around her neck. Applying some red lipstick, she grabbed her purse and leather coat and smiled when she noticed Savage looking her up and down.

"You doing that motherfucker." Savage stood up, cleaned himself. He had got a fresh blow out fade. On his wrist was a Cartier watch, and around his neck he wore his signature Savage Shit chain. His clothes were Dior everything, including his shades, which he grabbed off the bed and put on his face. Snatching up the Glock that had been beside it, he tucked it in his waistline and kissed Bubbles.

"Boy stop, we got to go," she told him, holding his hands. walking out the apartment.

They headed to the mall then to check out the building for her salon. When they hopped in Bubbles' Coupe, she was excited. Her face was beaming as she looked over at Savage.

"I love you too, Mrs. Bubbles," Savage told her, laying his chair back as Bubbles cut up the music, thinking, *I'm so happy*.

SKY

Sky was still going through the motions. Beauty's funeral was in a week. He saw on the news that Dave got smoked and was mad as shit that he ain't catch him first. Megan already put Sky on point about the nigga Squirrel and he was on it. He told her that they needed to do that shit tonight. Megan just smiled and told him that she had him.

Sky got dressed, grabbed his Glock, and stepped out the apartment. As soon he stepped in the hallway Tia stepped out.

"Come here, Sky," she called, inspecting him up and down.

"Naw, I'm on something," he told her and was walking down the step when she grabbed his arm. Sky snatched away, turning, looking at her like she was lunching.

"Boy, don't fake like you wasn't fucking me."

"Bitch, fuck you! And yo pussy trash, thot ass," Sky told her and marched out the building.

"Bitch, fuck yo dirty ass," Tia yelled, stomping back in her apartment with her feelings hurt.

CHINA

China and her buddy Kim were in the mall. They saw some heels on T.V. and China just had to have them. They were walking by the food court talking when China had to do a double take. It was Bubbles and Savage sitting down talking.

I knew it. Snake ass bitch, China said to herself.

"You okay girl? You look like you saw a ghost." Kim looked around, wondering what China was looking at.

"Nothing, girl... go head. I'ma meet you at the store." China told Kim, who shook her head and walked off. China walked a little closer, pulled out her phone, and began taking pictures.

She texted Tyson, letting him know she needed to see him

asap and that it was important. She smiled when he texted back.

Tyson: Just pull up baby!!

TIA

"This is D.C. News. Police are looking a Trey Gram and Steven Keys a.k.a Sky and Savage. Both are wanted for multiple murders and shootings. Authorities are offering a fifty-thousand-dollar reward for any information leading to an arrest. Please contact 1-800-CRIMESTOPPERS."

"Thot, huh?" Tia said to herself. "I got your thot, bitch," she said out loud as she called *Crimestoppers*.

TYSON

Tyson was in shock. *This snake ass bitch*, he mused as he looked at the pictures of Savage and Bubbles holding hands, pictures of them talking, hugging, and kissing.

"Thank you, baby, I got you." Tyson told China, giving her a kiss as he called Keem and Lil E. Soon as they answered he told them, "pull up, we got business to handle."

SKY AND RAVEN

After Sky and Raven left from picking out a tombstone for Beauty they stopped at Horse and Dickie's, getting 10 whiting fried fish with hot sauce and tater sauce on the side. Raven got a lemonade iced tea mixed. Sky didn't want no juice. They stopped at Rose's liquor and Sky bought himself a box of sheets, two packs of sour punch straws, and a bottle of Rosé.

"Tomorrow, I'ma go get Beauty tatted on me. Her funeral is in 4 days. Shit crazy… she gone on me like that." He told Raven, sitting the bag on the backseat.

"I'ma go with you. I got something that's going to make you feel a lil better. It's a surprise… you're going to get it when we get home." Raven teased him as he pulled off, heading to her house.

DETECTIVE ROB

"Everyone get in position, act normal. We're looking for a smoke gray Sport Range. I want officers at Raven's building. Secure the area because he's armed and dangerous, so proceed with caution," Detective Rob said in his walkie talkie.

He was sitting on Raven's porch steps in plain clothes watching as his team got in position. They were all in plain clothes, hoping the tip they received was right. They had already run in Raven's apartment finding guns and money. They had a good feeling this tip was right. Sky pulled in the parking lot, with Raven sucking his dick as he parked.

"This is real. He just rode in the parking lot. Stay in position until he walks in the Courts then take him." Detective Gram instructed in his walkie talkie, sitting in an unmarked car two cars down, pulling out his badge and Glock 17, getting ready.

Sky came in Raven's mouth soon as he parked, she swallowed it all, eyeballing him as she licked her lips.

"Come on Daddy. My pussy's soaking wet," she told him, grabbing the bags and food, hopping out the truck. Sky put his dick in his pants, grabbing the Glock off the floor.

"It's him. It's him… move!!" Detective Gram yelled, hopping out the car.

"Freeze! Freeze!" Sky heard and saw masks and plain clothed officers running towards him. He pushed Raven down, upped and got to clicking.

Boom! Boom! Boom! Boom! The first bullets hit Detective Gram in his head. He fell in the middle of the street.

"Nooo!" Raven screamed, watching officers open fire. Sky got hit, falling in the parking lot, gun landing beside him. All you heard were Raven's screams.

SAVAGE

Bubbles got a call from Whitegirl at 4 in the morning, telling her Savage's face was all over the news, and that Sky got shot up by the police tonight. Bubbles cut on the news, shaking her head, covering her hands over her mouth. She didn't want to wake Savage with more bad news, looking over at Savage, seeing he was sleeping peacefully. She rubbed her stomach, thinking about her unborn child.

"Savage," she called, kissing his lips, shaking him awake.

"Yeah, boo?" he answered, looking at her as he sat up, seeing tears racing down Bubbles' face.

"What's up, baby?"

"Sky got killed by the police."

"What?" Savage asked, shocked. His emotions were all over the place while gazing in Bubbles' face.

"It's all over the news. I'm sorry, baby," she said, hugging him as he let tears stream down his cheeks.

"They got your face all over the news, too. Wanted for murder. Baby, you're all over it. I'ma call my brother down in Miami. You got to get out of town," Bubbles told Savage, looking in his face.

"I'ma go to the shop and meet Whitegirl tomorrow. Give her instructions on what I want her to do while I'm gone."

"Aiight, twist up. Shit looking bad." Savage told Bubbles as he watched her climb out the bed, grabbing some gas and sheets.

Savage laid back on the bed with his eyes closed, thinking. *This is the life I choose. Savage Shit. R.I.P. Cat, Freaky, and Sky... see y'all when I get there.*

LIL E AND KEEM

Lil E and Keem were looking high and low for Bubbles, but no one had a line on her. Lil E and Keem were sitting in Checkers drive thru when Keem called Tyson. Shit was at a standstill. Tyson told him he was going to call him back. He hung up and called China, asking her what's up with Bubbles and her whereabouts. China told him she didn't know but told him Whitegirl was Bubbles' best friend and that she knew. Tyson hung up and called Keem back. Him and Lil E were sitting in Checkers' parking lot eating when Tyson called back. Keem answered on the first ring. Tyson told him Whitegirl's info and told him to grab the bitch and make her tell them where Bubbles was at.

"Say no more," Keem told Tyson and hung up. Keem looked at Lil E. "Work call," he said and pulled off.

BIG MIKE

Big Mike was watching the news. He saw that shit that happened to Sky. *Young niggas moving too fast. They don't know its levels to this shit. Savage is a good motherfucker; nothing like his father, but he stepped in the big leagues. Shit gets hard from there. Savage can't win when it's a ticker and the law on his heels.* Big Mike said to himself, his eyes on the news seeing Savage's face flash across the screen.

Big Mike looked down at Savage's picture again. Big Mike was the one that killed Big Savage. That's why he kept Savage so close, making sure he was okay because Big Mike always kept his enemies close. He grew to like Young Savage, but his time was running out. Big Mike's loyalty was with Tone. He was just trying to give Savage time to get out of town. Every car he sold him, Freaky, or Sky, he put a tracker in it. He been knew Bubbles' whereabouts and he knew where Savage was at right now. He was always one step ahead of the game. "You got two more hours," he said, staring at Savage's picture, hoping somehow Savage could hear him.

WHITEGIRL

Whitegirl talked to Bubbles early this morning and they made plans to meet at the salon at 11:30 a.m. Whitegirl took a shower and got dressed. She was in a good mood until she opened her front door, and two big ass guns were pointed in her face. Holding the guns were two masked men, forcing her in the house, tying her up, giving her a choice. "You either call Bubbles and bring her to us or we kill your stupid ass. Your choice." Lil E told her with his gun jammed in her face. Whitegirl was scared to death. She looked at the masked men's faces and made her choice.

BUBBLES AND SAVAGE packed all their shit. She kissed him and told him to be ready when she get back and left out the apartment. Keem had been sitting in a smacked-out Dodge Saturn since 10:30 a.m., waiting. Lil E was still at Whitegirl's apartment waiting on Keem to call; if Bubbles ain't show up, Lil E was smoking Whitegirl. Whitegirl was laying on the floor taped from her mouth to her ankles, praying she made it out alive.

BUBBLES' Coupe cruised up the block. Keem popped the trunk and started the car, sliding out. Bubbles had so much shit on her mind as she hopped out the car, she really didn't pay attention to Keem as he walked her way. Keem got close and smacked Bubbles as hard as he could with the Glock, breaking her face, and she fell on the sidewalk unconscious. Keem looked around before dragging her to the car and throwing her in the trunk. He hopped back in the car, pulling off.

SAVAGE

Savage was waiting on Bubbles. At 12:00 p.m. he called Bubbles and didn't get an answer, so he called Whitegirl and didn't get an answer. Savage was confused, wondering what the fuck was going on. He grabbed his 5th and Mac 11, putting the Mac in the bag with his money, leaving out the house to see what was going on, and getting out of town.

BUBBLES

Bubbles woke up with her face aching, ass naked, tied to a chair in the middle of a room. Her mouth was taped shut, ankles, wrists, and hands were cuffed.

"Welcome back, you snake bitch!" Tone said, rolling in the room in a wheel chair. Bubbles thought she saw a ghost while looking in his face.

"I know how the game go and it was my fault so I ain't fucked up about it. Now, you slipping, so I need to know everything you know about Savage, *now!*" Tone snatched the tape off her mouth.

Bubbles was crying. She thought about her unborn child, looked at Tone, and told him everything.

"Thank you," he offered before upping a 44 from under his thighs.

"Nooo!" she screamed.

Boom! Boom! Boom! Click. Click.

Tone pulled the trigger until all the bullets were gone. Blood was everywhere. The impact of the bullet broke her neck.

"Dumb ass bitch," Tone spat, rolling out the room, calling Tyson.

"Kill his aunt," he said, giving Tyson the address.

"I'm on it," Tyson told him and hung up, calling Lil E and Keem.

SAVAGE

Savage was riding through the city on high alert, Mac 11 on the passenger seat, Glock in his hand, ducked down watching everything. He rode by Bubbles' car wondering, *"where this bitch at? Fuck this! I got to get out of town,*

He pulled off just as his phone rang. He answered it as he did the speed limit up Florida Ave. "Yeah."

"Slim, what's up? Your face all over the news, Freaky got killed, Sky fucked around and killed the law, fuck you gon' do, slim?" Big Mike asked, putting plastic down on his entire floor.

"Shit bad. I'm bout to slide out to Miami. I got to get the fuck on," Savage told him, eyes on his surroundings.

"Pull up before you go. I got a spot you could lay low for a second. You know I got you… hurry up, doe. Don't make my shit hot," Big Mike told him and hung up, sitting at his desk. He grabbed his 357, surveilling the cameras and tracker while watching Savage.

"Two hours up, soldier. You stepped in the wrong pair of shoes," Big Mike said to himself, waiting on Savage to pull up.

Savage drove up to the car lot, parking. He sat the Glock on the floor and hopped out, jogging to the office. Soon as he stepped in, Big Mike shot him in the face.

Boom!

Savage fell on the plastic, body shaking. Big Mike looked down at him.

"My bad, Slim."

Boom! Boom! Boom!

He got him again, making sure he was dead. He looked at the Savage Shit chain and wrapped Savage up in plastic. Big

Mike pulled out his phone calling Tone. Soon as Tone answered Big Mike told him, "come clean this shit up."

"I'm retired, Tone. You on your own. I'm going home," Big Mike told him, hanging up and walking out the office.

Tone just smiled. "Clean up man," he said and looked at Tyson. "Savage is dead. Get somebody to get up Mike's joint to clean up."

"I'm on it," Tyson told him, walking out the room.

KEEM AND LIL E

"I got this," Lil E told Keem as he pulled up to Aunt J's house. Lil E hopped out the car and jogged to her apartment building. He tried the door and saw it was open. He creeped in, smelled crack in the air, and took his 5th off his hip and was walking when he saw two people in the bathroom.

Aunt J was on her knees, sucking the shit out Greg's dick, both their eyes were closed. Aunt J was fingering her pussy with the other hand. Greg still had on his jail release clothes. Lil E ran in the bathroom.

Boom!

He shot Greg at close range, then he turned the 5th on Aunt J, killing her before she could scream.

Boom!

Lil E turned and broke out the apartment, hopping in the car, telling Keem that Aunt J was in there sucking a nigga's dick as Keem did the dash up the block laughing.

<hr>

EPILOGUE

<hr>

*P*olice found Savage's and Bubbles' bodies floating in the Anacostia River two days later. Officers found Aunt J's and Greg's bodies. When Mya found out Greg was getting his dick sucked by a junkie, she was mad she ever gave him some pussy. When the paperwork came out and Megan found out Tia was the one that dropped the tip on Sky, she sliced her face and beat her half to death. Squirrel and Jones were still getting money. They turned the 22nd into a dope strip, getting bricks from Keem for the low. Only if they knew they were on that list. Tone popped back up from the dead and it was back to business.

Tyson gave China 150 bands and bought her a new Lex Coupe for her help. She still sucked Tyson's dick every chance she got. Dawn was hurt when she found out Savage got killed. She had a son that looked just like him, named him Trey Gram

Jr. but called him Baby Savage. She got Savage's portrait tatted on her back that said, *the realist nigga to ever live.* The streets still praised Savage and Sky.

Lil E didn't kill Whitegirl. She was happy to be alive and was fucked up about Bubbles, but she said, "better her than me. Life goes on."

Lil E and Keem were getting money up Montana with Pat, fucking all the bitches, doing them. They were lit!

Sky had died five times, but the doctors kept him alive. He was charged with seven bodies, including capital murder for killing Detective Gram.

Nook and Lil D got on the stand and told everything. Sky was looking at them niggas, thinking, *y'all some cowards.* Detective Rob was in the crowd at Sky's sentencing, mugging, wishing he could put a bullet in Sky's head. It took five years, but they found Sky guilty on all counts and sentenced him to 355 years.

Sky ain't give a fuck! He lost almost everything he ever loved anyway.

Raven had his son and stood by him even when he pushed her away. Her, Megan, and Lil Sky never missed a visit or phone call. He over 100 bands. Megan and Raven loved him forever.

"Aye, Lil Sky…" a C.O. called at 2:00a.m. "…you going to the feds this morning. Get your stuff. I'ma pop your cell for a shower in a couple minutes," the C.O. told him and walked away from the cell. Sky packed all his food, putting it in a net bag, and put all his soap and hygiene in another bag. After his cell popped open, he walked down to his man Sikey from farms cell, waking him up.

"Aye, Sikey, I'm gone, slim. I'm putting this food on your door, Moe."

"Aiight, slim. I see you when I get there," Sikey told em, nodding as Sky walked to the shower. Sky ain't really fuck with nobody but Sikey. Niggas knew what the fuck was up with him and respected Sky.

Sky got out the shower, got dressed, and left. He got transferred to OKA holdover, from there he went to Harrisburg, getting on a bus to Hazelton.

When he got to the jail and all the interviews were over, he didn't get to his unit until it was locked down. He saw people in their windows watching as he walked to a homie cell.

Gucci and Salaam were cellies. Gucci got five years for a Mac, and Salaam got 20 for crushing a nigga. They knew Sky got sentenced and was hoping he came down to Hazleton. They got the bus list that morning and saw his name. When Sky walked in the block everybody was hipped to the play. Gucci and Salaam saw him and stepped from the window, sharpening their knives up.

"What's up?" Sky greeted, walking in the homie cell.

"Shit, I'm Duck," the cellie told him, dapping Sky up. Duck was hipped to the play but knew the rules of this pen shit.

"You got a knife for me, Slim," Sky asked Duck as Duck handed him a care package.

"I ain't going lie. I'm out the way trying to make it to a F.C.I.," Duck told him as he got in the bed. Sky was tired from all that transferring, soon as he laid down, he went straight to sleep. The doors popped at 5:00a.m., and Duck was already up, teeth brushed out the cell.

Sky hopped off the top bunk, put on his shoes, and grabbed his toothbrush. He looked and saw Gucci and Salaam sliding in the cell. Salaam rushed Sky, stabbing him in his arm. Sky tried to fight but Gucci and Salaam were crushing him with their knives. Sky's body was getting weak as they stabbed and stabbed. He couldn't even hold his body no more, falling in the middle of the cell, leaking.

Gucci and Salaam flushed their knives and slid out the cell, shutting the door behind them.

Everybody in the unit knew what had just happened but was acting like everything was normal. Sky was choking on his own blood, his life flashed before his eyes. He saw the first person he ever killed. Sky saw Savage. He was trying to catch his breath as Raven's, his son's, Megan's, and Beauty's faces flashed across his face. Sky saw a light, his eyes rolling in the back of his head as he bled out on his cell floor.

The End

Did you enjoy the read?
Let us know how much by leaving us a review on Amazon
and Goodreads.

Keep reading for a preview of…
Coldhearted: Blood Stains And Broken Trust
By Lou Garden Price Sr.

CHAPTER 1

Newport Gardens Apartments

Brownsville, NY

Monday 3:00 AM

Five-year-old Sage Michael Thomas peeked through the slightly open door where he thought he might locate his mother, father, or maybe even both. He had been asleep on his pissy smelling airbed in the back of the apartment when he was awakened by several roaches crawling on his face, neck, and bare chest. Then, to top it off, a mouse had ran across his legs. They were all licking remnants of the peanut butter and jelly he had eaten the night before.

He was starving all over again and he was in luck because there they both were, on that old nasty brown living room sofa. Daddy was seated with his pants down and

Mommy's face was moving up and down in his lap – making wet eating noises. Well, to Sage it sounded like eating noises…

It was only 3:00 AM so it was still dark outside. That meant it was dark inside because Con Edison had turned out the lights. Sage heard Mommy and Daddy arguing about it the day before. In fact, Daddy had whooped her ass really bad. Afterwards, Daddy had given Sage the peanut butter and jelly to eat, no bread.

Sage knew not to bother Mommy while she was "eating" Daddy so he just tried to see better. The only light he had to see with was from two of those tall glass candles depicting pagan sketches of the so called *Virgin Mary* crying. Or *weeping* as the Catholics put it.

The faint candlelight flickered, casting a silhouette image of his mother slurping on his father, Big Kato. Arnesha, his mother, was still a hot piece at eighteen even though she'd had a five year old son at an early age and a dope habit. But that didn't matter because when she walked through the hood, nyggaz was still staring at that chocolate ass she was packing in them jeans. She was bad as fuck.

When Lindsey Lohan, Demi Lovato, and half of them bitches in Hollywood turn dopefiend, pillhead, alcoholic, or whatever, nyggaz still wanted to fuck them hos. The 'hood ain't no different except skin color and economic status. But the pussy remains the same.

"Arnesha! What – who da fuck was dat?" came from the

startled voice from the funky sofa he was getting his dick and balls licked on. "I thought you said no one else was here!"

"Don't just stand out there, boy," came the actual voice of his father from the far left. "C'mere!" Sage, confused, walked past the strange man on the sofa who Sage had initially thought was his father, wondering why Mommy was on her knees eating from him. Sage only wore a pissy pamper which his father took off of him, trashed it, and put on a fresh one.

"Can we go to another room?" the strange older Black man asked Arnesha in a whisper. "I'm so close."

"C'mon, baby," she said, starting to get up.

"Nah, bitch," Kato growled from where he sat in the kitchen. "Finish toppin' that greasy ass nygga off right there!" he demanded coldly.

"But the lil nygga," the trick protested, but only for a moment.

"Pay attention to me, honey," she said as she took him back into her warm wet mouth. She was so thick, her chocolate titties were out and he held her head as he hardened fully again. "*Mmm! Glbb!* Mmm…"

"You see ya mama, son?" Kato whispered into Sage's little ear so that neither she nor her trick could hear him narrate what was happening. "She earnin' money for the lights to come on… and so you can have some milk, bread, eggs, and cereal. You want Captain Crunch?"

Sage nodded while keeping an eye on his Mother.

"See, son," Kato continued on. "Truth is, I went to jail and come home to a dopefiend whore. She tells me you prolly ain't even mine. That made me feel so evil I wanted to kill her and you."

Kato, whose real name was Titus White, was no slouch in the streets, but Arnesha was a ho and that reflected on him. Ever since they were both in the 7th Grade together they'd been in love. But when she'd gotten pregnant that changed everything. That pressure, coupled with the fact that neither of them were the brightest students to come out of Wingate High School, Kato had resorted to selling crack. Naturally, that eventually landed him in jail.

During his stay on Rikers Island, Arnesha had began popping Zannies and OxyContin's. Not long after that, she'd started snorting heroin. To support her growing habit she'd sold pussy. Subsequently, Kato was released to see her and Sage living in complete and total squalor at the notorious Noble Drew Ali Plaza Projects on New Lots and Mother Gaston Avenues in Brownsville.

In any event, Kato was a fearless stickup kid by trade so it didn't take long for him to move Arnesha and Sage into Newport Gardens Apartments on Lott and Rockaway Avenues. It was around that time when Kato's probation had been violated and he'd been returned to Rikers Island for a few months.

This time, when he was released, the streets were laughing even harder behind his back because another man had emerged as a possible father for Sage. Now, this ho not only fucked half the whole Brownsville but now Sage was "probably not" his son?

The sticky wet slurping sounds continued.

Glbb! Glbb! Mmm! The loud breathing and her sloppy sucking and moaning sounds had now filled the entire room. The candlelights seemed to burn brighter. *Glbb! Glbb! Mmmm, Mmmm!*

SWWOOOSSSHHH!! A sound similar to a wire hanger slicing through the air at 100 mph. And then, right behind that a flat: TTHHUUMMPP! sound. Something heavy hitting the floor behind the sofa. But Arnesha was currently throating her trick as if her life depended on it. She thought her son had dropped something and ignored it. All that mattered was the dick in her mouth and the $50 he had paid. She was trying to finish him off and get herself a fix.

However, Arnesha felt the moisture of a misty like spray hitting her face and forearm as if it were raining and a window was open nearby. Then, she realized that one second the tricks member was raging hard and then the next he was instantly flaccid. "What the hell, man?!" She complained.

She looked up at his face and she jumped backwards, screaming as she fell onto her ass, knocking over the littered coffee table! The trick's entire head was missing!

To her left stood Big Kato, a large 6 foot 2 inch, 240 pound young man with curly hair and no facial hair. He wielded a long, sharp, machete in his right hand with blood leaking off the blade. Arnesha trembled and screamed bloody

murder when she looked over to her right and saw the trick's head, its eyes open, staring directly at her!

"OH, MY FUCKIN GOD!!!" She yelled and then started screaming.

"Shut yo ho ass up!!" Kato boomed, pointing the machete down at her.

He turned to Sage and for an extended, silent, moment he stared at him. Perhaps he'd contemplated killing him. Kato had lost it. He had the look of a madman in his eyes.

"Every man needs his dignity, Sage," Kato declared to the boy. "Remember dat."

He used his cellphone to pull up Youtube. Once he was filming himself he said, "Aight this must be how the white folks, school shooters, and terrorists do it huhn? Well, everybody, I just beheaded this dirty mufucka… as he was gettin' head by a ho I thought I loved. Take a look…"

He showed the world the decapitated head as best as he could with the darkness in the room. "See? This is my machete, my kill. This is my… I think he's my son. This bitch is his mother – a whore. She fucked all of my boys, I'm a laughingstock. A man needs his fuckin' dignity. So this is how I'm goin' out."

With that, he sat the phone down so it could record his next move. Then, he turned the machete on Arnesha…

When the cops arrived, from the 73rd precinct, he lunged at them with the machete raised in one hand while carrying Sage with the other, as a human shield! He was cut down immediately with a burst of semi-automatic gunfire!

"Hold your fire!!" a yell came.

"Hold your fire!!" someone repeated.

"He has a child!!" a ESU Sergeant bellowed.

Cops discovered that the child had also been shot and that sent everyone into an even greater panic! Sage was rushed to the hospital!

But not even the Youtube video could have prepared them for the shock and horror of what was inside of the apartment.

CHAPTER 2

Newport Gardens Apartments

Brownsville, New York

Monday 6:00 AM

THERE WAS BLOOD EVERYWHERE.

Absolutely everywhere. The lead homicide detective on the case was Camille Vasquez and as she walked inside of the first-floor apartment, and stood in the center of the living room, that's what she was observing.

The body on the sofa, the headless male with his pants around his ankles, still sitting upright. His head on the floor, eyes open, genitals on full display.

The mother, also brutally mutilated, hands missing, feet severed, plus her head had been chopped off. "Her eyes are closed," Camille muttered.

"What's that, Cammie?" Detective Brad Wannamaker queried as he entered, zipping up a white vinyl protective suit.

Camille stood upright, glancing at the good looking 6 foot tall blond veteran detective. Then, indicating the decapitated heads, "The Black male here, his eyes are open because he never seen the blade comin'. And our female victim here… well, her eyes are closed because she seen it comin'. He chopped off her arms which she used to try to shield herself. *Dios mio.* Imagine seein' your own limbs chopped off and your last thing is squeezing your eyes shut as the machete comes down on your neck like a guillotine."

Camille was only a five year veteran before being assigned to homicide recently. However, it had become clear to the Unit Sergeant, and other detectives inside of the Division, that she had a superior talent for understanding crime scenes and solving murders.

She looked Puerto Rican but she was actually Argentinian. She had shoulder length brown hair, silvery eyes, and very pretty. She was average height, for a woman, and had a provocative figure. She cleared everyone at the crime scene – who shouldn't be there – out.

"Our perp is dead," Cam sighed as she filmed with a small handheld digital camera. "Mom's fellating the BM deceased on the sofa as Dad watches. At some point, the toddler awakes and enters through this door."

Indicating the kitchen table she states, "Dad sits there watching mom perform… judging from the squalor of this place she's a crackhead or dopefiend. We know Titus White is a thug and gang banger. Arnesha here was the boy's mother."

The two homicide detectives stared at each other as Sergeant Matthew French, Lt. Maury Coviello, and Captain Joe Vaughn entered unexpectedly. They slowly looked around and the Captain spoke first.

"This entire fucking this is captured on Youtube!" he boomed with an explosive hand gesture. "And now it's being watched by every schmuck with a cellphone or internet all over the goddamned planet!"

Captain Vaughn removed his hat and handkerchief and wiped the rivulets of sweat from his bald head and face. He was a light skinned Black man with a thin mustache and broad torso. He shook his head as he looked around.

"How does it go unreported that a small boy is living in a dump like this?" Vaughn queried no one in particular as he did a walk through. "Is this a generator?"

Camille Vasquez nodded. "Yes, sir. There's no electricity so our own crime lab had to use generators to light it up."

The Captain inspected the air mattress and room the boy slept in and grimaced at the pungent stench of urine and feces he smelled. "My lord. Does everyone here understand the pressure we're about to face?"

Sergeant French, Lieutenant Coviello, Camille, and her partner listened to Captain Vaughn attentively, nodding their heads yes.

"The beheadings are one thing," Vaughn explained. "First

we got a guy out on early probation. They're gonna holler about how he got a low plea deal when Titus White is – or was – a known home invader. Then they're gonna go after the D.A. again for allowing this child to live like this because the probation department *had to* visit before Titus was released, correct?"

"Supposedly," Coviello commented.

"The Department of Socal Services will get ripped for not stepping in," the Captain went on. "And when this knife-wielding maniac charged at officers how did we not see the fucking kid he was carrying as a human shield?!"

"Captain, sir?" Camille spoke up. "Not tryin' to justify… but the guy had a *machete* as he charged. Officers *had to* open fire," she stated sarcastically.

"Well…" the Captain spoke slowly. "After all that kid has lost, let's hope he doesn't lose his life."

"What's his status?" Camille asked.

"He's in surgery," the Captain reported. "Last word I got he lost a lot of blood and… five years old. Shot by the NYPD. Damned shame," Vaughn shook his head solemnly. But it was an act. The same dog and pony show for 99.9999933% of AmeriKKKan Police. Especially in New York. The NYPD's the most racist and most murderous fucking cops in the world. They're the modern day Gestapo whose methodology has been exported to every city and town in the USA with Black and Latinos in it. Just take a look back… even before Eric Garner…

Anthony Ramon Baez, December 22, 1994 (murdered by a bitch ass Bronx cop); Abner Louima, August 9, 1997, beaten by coward Brooklyn cops, kicked in the nuts, and sodomized- up the anus- with a fucking toilet plunger); he lived but might as well be dead after that shit. Amadou Diallo, February 4, 1999- shot 41 times by 4 Bronx cops.

NYPD hates Black people. If Sage dies, in a situation such as this it's just another nygga dead to those evil motherfuckers.

CHAPTER 3

Montefiore Hospital
Bronx, New York
Monday 7 PM

Daphne Garcia stood outside of Sage Michael Thomas's room looking in through the window. He had been out of emergency surgery for only a few hours where doctors labored well into the day to stabilize him. He had started the day out at Brooklyn's Brookline Hospital but once he was out of surgery he was sent to the Children's Trauma Unit at Montefiore Hospital in the Bronx.

Daphne was a Social Worker assigned by The Family Court of Brooklyn to oversee the case file while she stood outside looking in at Sage. When she'd first been told she had to drive all the way up to the Bronx she'd been annoyed. Her supervisor had told her something about the case but there were so many like it, she had become numb.

That attitude may sound cruel and insensitive for a woman in her position to have but there were so many school shootings, children dying by "stray" bullets, cases of severe child abuse, neglect, car accidents, and so much more Daphne sees or watches on the news. Like many people, she's become desensitized from tragedy. It happens so much. Especially in New York City.

"Excuse me," a small blond woman appeared behind Daphne. The lab coat she wore had a nametag on it saying that she was a doctor.

"Yes, hi," Daphne greeted her.

"Doctor Kim Willow, is he your family?"

Daphne shook her head no. "Daphne Garcia, Department of Social Studies, Emergency Division."

Dr. Willow nodded and they both took a moment to observe the small brown skinned toddler laying atop the bed with all the tubes and wires going into and out of him. He wore a small oxygen mask. There was a feeding tube down his nose, taped to his face.

"What's his outlook?" Daphne inquired. "Day to day?"

"I wish," Willow said. "Try more like moment to moment. He's in excruciating pain for a child his size. That alone may kill him."

Daphne gave her the file her supervisor had emailed her. "I've had some of the worst cases you could ever think of involving children… Child abandonment, child abuse, sexual abuse, cases of incest, abduction recovery, and even child abuse deaths where kids have died from injuries, neglect, and malnutrition. But none where a toddler was used as a human shield by a father with a machete. And-"

Daphne choked up. It was too much.

Dr. Willow nodded. "You okay?"

They sat down on a cushioned bench nearby as the ICU nurse entered Sage's room. The petite blond haired doctor handed Daphne some tissue to wipe her tears.

"I don't normally see DSS people cry," Willow told her. "You guys are usually such a hardened bunch."

Daphne Garcia was normally unfazed by all of the pain, death, and tragedy around her life. The 5 feet 4 inch tall, great looking, Dominicana-Boriqua woman of 28 had been born and raised in the Bronx. She had very long hair which was naturally black but was now red. Her sister Maria was a hairstylist. As young girls, they had both aspired to be salon owners, hair & nail stylists, but Daphne ended up obtaining her Bachelor's degree in Sociological Studies and becoming a social services counselor in Brooklyn.

"Where I came from you see so much you choose this work to try to help," Daphne said, tears still in her eyes. "But it's days like this when you realize how helpless you really are. I mean what do you do for a five year old lying there, fighting for his life because his father killed mom, then killed himself, and he was shot by police?"

Dr. Willow lightly patted her on her right knee. "You *pray*. And if you don't pray, then hope."

"If you were to bet your next paycheck on whether he'll make it, would you?" Daphne asked her.

Willow shook her head. "I would not. He's had a great deal of trauma. One bullet shattered his left ankle. He was also hit in the lower abdomen where he suffered intestinal ruptures but no vital organ damage. What worries us the most is that he is so severely underweight. He's five but looks two or three. I mean, god, what were these parents doing?!" she lamented.

Daphne knew it was more of a statement than a question, but she said, "The mother was an eighteen year old drug addict, living in poorly kept low income housing. His father was an abusive animal, in and out of jail, with multiple women under his belt. There are a number of theories of why or what made him snap. We'll learn more in the days and weeks to come," the social worker offered.

Dr. Willow was at a loss for words. Dr. Willow finally said, "Where will he go? I mean… that leg. He'll need therapy. Specialized care. Not to mention his mental healthcare."

"I'll try to locate next of kin," Daphne replied. "No one has come forward yet."

Dr. Willow's jaw dropped. "No one has called social services after this shit has been broadcasted around the world? No aunts? Uncles? No grandparents?"

"Not on call or email. "Daphne shook her head no to every question. She liked the doctor even more now that she cussed.

"However, before I leave I'll meet with the social services here at the hospital and leave my contact information in case someone pops up. But as of yet, we have nothing."

Dr. Willow looked flabbergasted. "Dear God... no offense to you but I have zero faith in the foster care system."

Daphne scoffed. "No offense taken. Me neither. I *abhor* bad parents and loathe bad foster care parents even more because of several reasons. One, I question a lot of their motivations for even becoming foster parents to begin with. It's a for-profit system for another."

"But to take on a kid for a *welfare check*?"

"Girl, please," Daphne waved her off like she was talking nonsense. "It's a *hustle*. Especially now. Obama changed it. There's the welfare check, these parents know how to manipulate daycare benefits, they use these kids to defraud food banks, hopping from one to another so they can sell the food stamps to drug dealers, and store owners and pocket the cash. The more kids the better. They get *Section Eight* Housing and I mean enormous, nice, houses or apartments! As the older kids get older they are used in many cases to raise the younger... I'm telling you it's a game and most play it well. Until they get caught."

"And it's the kids who pay," Dr. Willow said.

Daphne nodded. "I've seen child abuse, sex abuse, sex *trafficking* where the foster mother was pimping out her underaged girls."

Dr. Willow shook her head. "Here? In New York?"

Daphne nodded. "What writer was it that said: *New York; a city inhabited by savages.*"

"Rogers? Dee Brown of *On Wounded Knee*?" Dr. Willow offered.

"Brown," Daphne agreed. Then, sighing, she stood up and handed Willow her card. "My cell number is there, too. Please give me a call if there are any changes in his improvement… or, god forbid if we have to send the poor guy to potters field."

"You mean to Hart Island," Dr. Willow said. "The World's largest mass grave."

With a solemn look, Daphne said, "That's the place."

She went into the room with Willow and bent down to whisper into his ear: "*Mejor, chicito. Get better. Fight. Stay strong. You've come this far. Why stop now?*"

Then, patting him lightly on the leg, feeling his warmth she hesitated.

"Daphne?" Dr. Willow looked at her.

"Yeah?"

The two women looked at each other and it was like they *knew*. Daphne had tears.

"I'll get another chair brought in," Willow said.

"That'll be great," Daphne took the cushioned chair that sat in the corner and pulled it up next to the bed.

Dr. Willow returned with a dark haired male medical assistant following her carrying a large orange cushioned chair. He sat it down on the opposite side of the bed and stood by.

No more words needed to be exchanged. Sage Michael Thomas would not be alone whether he – by some miracle – made it past the severity of his injuries or if he succumbed to them.

Daphne wrapped his small hand around her fingers so he had the energy of human contact. Dr. Willow did the same, bringing a smile to Daphne's face.

Available Now on Amazon

OTHER BOOKS BY

URBAN AINT DEAD

Tales 4rm Da Dale

By **Elijah R. Freeman**

The Hottest Summer Ever

By **Elijah R. Freeman**

Despite The Odds

By **Juhnell Morgan**

Good Girl Gone Rogue

By **Manny Black**

Hittaz 1, 2 & 3

Coldhearted

By **Lou Garden Price, Sr.**

Charge It To The Game 1 & 2

A Summer To Remember With My Hitta

By **Nai**

A Setup For Revenge

By **Ashley Williams**

Ridin' For You

By **Telia Teanna**

The State's Witness 1 & 2

By **Kyiris Ashley**

Stuck In The Trenches

By **Huff Tha Great**

The Swipe

By **Toōla**

BOOKS BY
URBAN AINT DEAD's C.E.O

<u>Elijah R. Freeman</u>

Triggadale 1, 2 & 3

Tales 4rm Da Dale

The Hottest Summer Ever

Murda Was The Case 1 & 2

Follow

Elijah R. Freeman
On Social Media

FB: Elijah R. Freeman

IG: @the_future_of_urban_fiction

www.ingramcontent.com/pod-product-compliance
Lightning Source LLC
Chambersburg PA
CBHW072123300726

48975CB00003B/906